#1 *NEW YORK TIMES* BESTSELLING AUTHOR

JESSICA SORENSEN

Raveling You

a Novel

For information:

jessicasorensen.com

Cover Design: Mae I Design

www.maeidesign.com

Raveling You (Unraveling, #2)

ISBN: 978-1505477399

Chapter 1

Lyric

"I think we should get one of the dead ones." A smile curls at my lips as I pluck a brown pine needle off a tree veering toward eternal death. "Just think about it. We'd be the only ones in the entire neighborhood with a brown Christmas tree. We'd really stand out amongst the masses."

Ayden's lips quirk as he flicks a tree branch. "As much as I'd love to let you have your way, I doubt Lila or your mom would be too thrilled if we came home with a fire hazard for a Christmas decoration."

"It wouldn't be the first time. One time, Uncle Ethan and my dad brought home this baby pine tree that had hardly any needles after Aunt Lila told them to bring home the cutest Christmas tree they could find." I tug my beanie lower onto my head and zip my jacket all the way up to my chin. "They thought they were so funny, but she was so mad she threw the tree in the fireplace."

Even though we live in San Diego, where it never snows, the December air has a nip to it. We're at a tree lot, trying to figure out which tree is considered "flourishing." The area smells like forest and pine nuts, and the red and green twinkly lights on the sign and fence glimmer across our faces, evidence that the holidays are spritzed everywhere; trees, yards, streets, stores.

I generally enjoy the spirit of Christmas, but after attending the funeral for Ayden's brother, Felix, yesterday, this year seems less cheery. Ayden hardly showed any emotion at the graveyard. I held his hand through the eulogy, and he gripped on for dear life, as if the connection was the only thing keeping him on his feet. I tried my best to keep it together for him, to stay upbeat.

Still am.

"She set the angel tree topper on fire, too," I continue when Ayden doesn't crack a smile. "You should have seen how the dress went up in flames. Looked like a little devil toward the end of it."

"You're so full of it," he says with a ghost of a smile. "But thank you."

"For what?"

"For trying."

His words don't make me feel any better, since he still appears depressed.

I tip my head up to the night sky and spot a shooting star glimmering across the sky. Under my breath, I utter a wish that Ayden will be able to overcome all of his obstacles. Not just with the passing of his brother, but with his sister not being at the funeral. No one will give him any information about where she is, either. He's frustrated, although he rarely complains about his hardships—never has.

On top of all of that, he's dealing with a tremendous amount of pressure from the police to seek therapy to try to restore his memories. He's conflicted with what he feels is right and wrong; not helping means turning his back on his brother's memory and helping means facing the demons of his past.

Although he has never flat out told me the specific details of what he can recollect about his time before foster care, I've come up with my own speculations, and all are horrible. The homemade tattoo they branded on his flesh tells me how mistreated he was while he was held captive.

"What do you think about this one?" Ayden draws my attention back to him.

He's standing by a tall, puffy tree propped against the fence.

I move beside him and angle my chin up to stare at the tip of the towering tree. "It might be a little excessive and will probably barely fit in your living room. Remember how super frustrated Aunt Lila was with Uncle Ethan last year when he brought home that one that was too big for the living room? The top nearly touched the damn ceiling, and there was hardly any room for the angel."

"Yeah, I forgot about that." His frown deepens. "I guess you're right. It'll probably be better to get a smaller one this year." His head falls forward and strands of black hair drift into his dark eyes.

He's so beautiful and sad, like the haunting portrait my mother painted of her mother's grave surrounded by black mist and bleeding rose petals. I wanted to cry every time I looked at it. She ended up selling it for a ton of money. Guess people have a thing for depressing and slightly morbid stuff.

I need to cheer him up somehow.

Come on, Lyric. You can do better.

I place my hands on my hips. "All right, dude, what's with the poutiness?"

He gives me a sidelong glance. "Dude? Are we really going back to that?" A playful tone edges into his voice. *Finally.*

"Um, hello. You will always be my dude, even when we're super old." I flash him my pearly whites. "You'll be all badass—old with a cane and a hunch, but rockin' your boots and black, studded clothes. And, sometimes, you'll even smile and make all the ladies in the old folks' home giggle like they did when they were sixteen. You'll totally be grandpa dude worthy."

Laughter escapes his lips. "So, you're putting me in an old folks' home, huh? Nice to know where I'm headed."

"Yeah, well, I had to. Your cane was cramping my hot Grandma swagger."

His lips twitch as a full smile threatens to break through. "Oh, my God. I would love to know how you come up with this shit."

"No, you wouldn't." I put the tip of my two fingers to my temple. "Trust me, you're way better off not knowing what goes on in here." When he laughs again, I dare ask, "So, are you going to tell me why you got all sad puppy eyes when I said this tree might not be the way to go?"

"It's not a big deal." He skims over the trees then nods his head to a shorter one near the entrance of the tree shop. "We should probably go for one like that."

I catch his sleeve before he can wander off. "No way. We're totally getting one of the tall ones."

"Nah. You were right. They're too tall."

"Nope, they're just right. Besides, Uncle Ethan will make it work, and he'll love every second doing so. And then we can get me this bad boy," I point at an equally tall and fluffy tree leaning beside the one Ayden picked out, "so we can be twins." I waggle my eyebrows at him. "And we both know how much you love being just like me."

"Yep, it's my secret wish," he finally, FINALLY jokes back. "In fact, every night when I go to sleep, I look out my window, find a shooting star, and beg it to please let me wake up and be exactly like Lyric."

"Ha, ha." I aim a finger at him and force a falsetto laugh. "I knew it."

"You are such a weirdo." He's totally smiling a big, ol' grin from ear to ear.

"Yeah, but a weirdo that you're so in love with." As soon as I say it, I instantly want to retract it.

Ayden massages the back of his neck tensely, looking

everywhere except at me.

Can you say awkward?

It used to not be this complicated between us, but that was before the kissing and touching we did in my car. Since then, stuff between us has gotten slightly uncomfortable if certain subjects come up, like love.

I don't feel bad about it at all, though. Ayden doesn't even tell the Gregorys he loves them. I honestly don't think he can say that word and mean it, not yet anyway. There are several things he can't do, like allow anyone to touch him more intimately than holding a hand or a hug. While we have kissed twice, our lip-locking has come to a grinding halt ever since his brother's death. He's not cold toward me—he cuddles and holds my hand more than he used to. I think his brother's mysterious death has messed with his mind, though, because that dark place he forgot about for over three years is trying to reenter his life.

"Okay, this weirdo right here is getting hungry." I rub my tummy. "So, how about we load up these lovely trees and stop to get a burger on the way home before I starve to death?"

"Fine, but only if you let me pay this time." He relax-

es, and so do I. "You always pay."

I link arms with him. "Okay, I'll let you pretend to be the man for tonight." When his lips tug upward, I press on, "Man, I'm so funny. What would you do without me?"

He stares at me, dead serious. "I honestly have no idea." With a sigh, he wiggles his arm from mine and gently drapes it over my shoulder. A simple gesture but out of the ordinary for him. "Come on. Let's go pay for the trees and get you your burger so we can get back. Otherwise, we'll be late for band practice."

We pay for the trees and load them in the back of my Uncle Ethan's truck, who really isn't my uncle, not by blood anyway. Uncle Ethan and Aunt Lila are just close to my parents, best friends to be exact. I've known them since I was born and sometimes call them aunt and uncle.

Once we hop into the cab and pull out onto the road, Ayden turns on the radio, flipping on some Brand New. I've learned over the last year of our friendship that his music choices portray how he feels. Tonight, he's stuck in his own head. I'd ask him what he's thinking about, but I know him well enough to understand he more than likely won't tell me.

The Christmas tree shop is about a ten-minute drive

from our neighborhood, so after we pick up some takeout, we still arrive home with a decent amount of time to spare before we have to leave for band practice.

The moon is a glowing orb and the stars sprinkle like pixie dust across the sky. A scenic night to be decorating the house, which is exactly what Uncle Ethan is doing when we pull up.

"What's with the inflatable Santa?" Ayden nods at Ethan who's inflating a massive Santa near the border of where our properties meet. "Last year, he put it that close to your house, too."

"It's because my dad's afraid of them." I unbuckle my seatbelt. "I guess he got stuck under one during a teenage prank gone wrong. Every year, Uncle Ethan puts it up to torture him. They're so crazy and weird, maybe weirder than me."

"Yeah, but it's nice, I guess. To have Christmas traditions like that, something you guys have done for years." He silences the engine and unfastens his seatbelt.

Suddenly, his deal with the big tree makes sense. He wants to keep tradition by getting a large one like the Gregorys did last year during his first Christmas with the family. He was so quiet back then, and I was awkward, trying to push him out of his comfort zone. I wanted so much for him to be my friend. This year, I want him to be more than that. But with what he's going through, I can't expect anything more than friendship.

"You know, my mom is having one of her holiday art shows like she did last year on New Year's Eve," I tell Ayden as I open the door to get out. "We could go again, but this time we can try sneaking off with a few glasses of eggnog. Get buzzed. Add to the tradition."

"I thought you were going to go to that party with Sage?" Ayden's brow arches as he glances at me. "That one Maggie invited you guys to."

Sage is the drummer of our band. With his blue-dyed hair, multiple piercings, and tattoos, he fits the part of what most people think a drummer should look like. After two months of jamming with him, I'm still deciding if he's a walking cliché or just an expressive person.

"Well, she invited you, too, silly. But I think the art show would end up being more fun. Besides, parties still make me uneasy. And I could very well run into William there."

William is the guy who assaulted me and attempted to

rape me at a party a few months ago. Thankfully, I was able to get away before he got too far, but the thought of being near him makes me uneasy.

"You shouldn't worry about running into him," Ayden says. "*He's* the one who should be worried, not you."

"I know, but unfortunately, that's not the way it works. I saw him at school after he did his community service. The douche had the nerve to grin at me."

"I want to punch him in the face," Ayden growls through gritted teeth, gripping onto the steering wheel, his knuckles turning white.

"You already did that." I gently touch his arm, hoping to calm him down. "We just need to move on now. Stewing in what he did only gives him more power."

"You got that from my therapist."

"Yeah. He said that to me when I went to visit him."

I went to one therapy session after what happened with William, mainly because my parents needed to know my head was okay. Talking about what happened was thera-peutic, but not enough for me go to weekly visits like Ayden does.

"So, what do you say?" I ask, clasping my hands in

front of me. "Does an art show sound New Year's Eve worthy? Pretty please, say yes."

"Sure. An art show sounds good." He offers me a small, grateful smile. "But only because you said pretty please."

"Awesome." I shove the door open all the way, and a chilly breeze gusts inside the cab. "I'm going to go tell my dad to come get the tree. Then I'm going to take a shower. I smell like pine needles and greasy burgers, not a great combo." I pause before I jump out. "Are you driving tonight or am I?"

"I can..." He appears distracted, his attention on the garage ahead of us.

"Hey, are you okay?" I search for what he might be looking at, maybe hidden in the shadows, but I don't see anything.

"Yeah, I'm fine." His gaze finds mine and he blinks dazedly. "I was just thinking about some stuff I have to do tonight."

"Anything you want to talk about?" I swing my legs over the edge of the seat to hop out of the truck.

He shakes his head then forces a stiff smile. "I'll go take care of the trees and then head over to your house in about a half an hour."

I suppress a sigh, jump out of the truck, and close the door. Giving a quick wave to Ayden, I round the fence between our driveways and enter the warmth of my home.

My dad is in the kitchen when I walk in. He has a notebook in his hand, intently reading one of the pages as he nibbles on a cookie. His blond hair is sticking up, and he looks stressed out.

"Yo, Daddy-O." I slam the door with an excessive amount of force to scare him.

He jumps and drops the cookie on the floor. "Jesus Christ, Lyric." He shakes off his jumpiness and scoops up the cookie from the hardwood floor. "You scared the shit out of me."

"That's what I was going for." I unzip my jacket and grab a cookie off the plate in the middle of the table. "Nice hair by the way. Did you just get out of bed? Or were you going for that bedhead/fauxhawk look all the cool kids are wearing nowadays?"

He places his palm on the top of his head, flattening his hair down. "Is it really that bad?" When I nod, he puffs out a frazzled exhale. "I was just going through some things for work, and I guess I took my stress out on my hair." He pulls out a chair and sits down at the table.

I rest my arms on the back of a chair and lean over the table to get a glimpse of what's on the pages. "Anything I can help with?"

He fans through the pages then rakes his fingers through his hair, making the ends stand right back up and solving the culprit of the bedhead/fauxhawk look. "Nah, it's just club stuff I'm trying to figure out."

"Like what?"

His brows elevate. "You really want to hear about my business problems?"

I stuff the rest of the cookie into my mouth. "That all depends on if it has to do with the music business side of it."

"It does." He seems hesitant to embellish.

I drop down in the chair across from him. "Then lay it on me. I'm all ears."

"Okay, but you have to promise me one thing," he says with reluctance. "That you won't mention your band at all during the conversation."

"My lips are sealed." I drag my fingers across my lips, pretending to zip them up.

His mouth is set in a firm frown, as if the last thing he wants to do is discuss whatever he's stressing about. "It's about one of the bands I had lined up for the opening." He waits for me to go back on my word and react, and I almost do, but forcefully smash my lips together, instead. "The lineup's pretty cool, but one of the opening bands backed out at the last second, so my big plan to carry it out all day isn't going to be possible. I mean, I still have a lot of good ones lined up." He reads over a scribbled list of band names. "I just wanted seven total." He flips the page, muttering nonsense, while I struggle not to put my two cents in. "It really isn't a big deal, except that it is since the flyer and advertisement said there'd be seven bands."

I raise my hand in the air like I'm in grade school.

"And it's too late notice to find someone else. The opening is less than three weeks," he carries on, ignoring my raised hand. "I'm already in the lineup, and I'll be way too busy making sure things run smoothly to try to take on two sets."

I bounce up and down in my chair, waving my hand in front of his face. "Hello? Can't you see my hand?"

"I can." He closes the notebook. "And I know what

you're going to say. The answer is no, though."

My shoulders slump as I plant my ass back in the chair. "No to what?" I fake pout. "You haven't even heard what I'm going to say."

"But I already know what you're going to say."

"How so?"

"Because we share the same musical DNA, and twenty-five years ago, if I'd been sitting in your spot, I'd have asked the same question you want to ask right now."

I jut out my lip. "You're cruel."

"No, I'm being a good father." He shoves his notebook aside and rests his elbows on the table. "There's no way I'm going to let my seventeen-year-old daughter and her band play at a club with a bunch of hardcore rock bands."

"FYI, I'm almost eighteen." I cross my arms and slump back in the chair. "You haven't even heard us play yet. Maybe we're as good as those hardcore rock bands."

"It's not that I doubt your ability, Lyric. I've heard you play and sing behind closed doors. You're fucking talented." I start to beam. "But…" he adds, and I frown—there's always a but— "it takes a lot of prep time to play onstage. And I'm not just talking about practice time, but mental prepping."

Aw, my parents and their concern for my mental stability. The worry seems to be expanding, too, ever since Ayden went into his depressive state, as if they believe we're so in sync I'll shut down with him.

I narrow my eyes, getting defensive. "Hey, we're ready. More than ready. We fucking rock."

"Yeah, but I'm not sure I'm ready for you to grow up that fast yet." He scoots the chair away from the table to stand up. "The environment at these things ... it's intense."

"You played when you were my age," I argue. "Maybe not at clubs, but I've heard the stories about the parties you and Mom went to back in the day."

He gapes at me. "When did you hear stories?"

I rise from my chair. "Every time you, Mom, Uncle Ethan, and Aunt Lila get drunk, you sit in the living room and reminisce about the good old days. And you're really loud drunks." I snatch up another cookie and stride for the doorway.

"Lyric, please don't be upset," he pleads. "This has nothing to do with your ability."

"Of course it doesn't." I pop a chunk of the cookie into my mouth and raise my chin in confidence. "You've never really heard me sing. And I mean *really* sing. Because, if you did, you'd be overlooking your overprotective father thing you've got going on right now and let me own your opening."

He opens his mouth to say something, but no words come out. I've struck him speechless, which was exactly what I was hoping for, even though I'm totally being over-confident. Our band doesn't even have a name, at least one we all agree on, and we haven't played anywhere other than inside the four walls of Sage's garage. But confidence can carry you a long way. Believe in yourself, and other people will, too. At least, I'm hoping that's where this con-versation goes.

"And P.S.," I add, "a fantabulous Christmas tree is waiting in the back of Uncle Ethan's truck for you."

I walk out of the kitchen, leaving my father to stew in his thoughts, and go upstairs to take a shower. Afterward, I blow-dry my long, blonde hair straight, apply some kohl eyeliner, and then tug on a pair of black torn jeans and a red shirt. It's nearing eight o'clock by the time I finish getting ready.

I glance out the window at Ayden's bedroom. The lights are on, with the curtains shut. He's kept them consistently closed for the last week, and I often wonder if he's hiding something behind them. I could be overanalyzing his distant behavior, but I don't know... There have been moments since his brother died when he'll suddenly announce he has to go home, even if we're in the middle of a movie or at band practice. He always goes into his bedroom and locks the door; at least, that's what I heard Aunt Lila whispering to my mother the other day.

"I'm getting worried," she said while they were unloading Christmas presents from the car, "about what he's doing in there. Like, maybe drugs."

They didn't know I was listening from the garage, but I stepped out and gave them my input. "He's not on drugs. You guys are overreacting. He probably just needs his space." I didn't bother mentioning that Ayden and I technically get high on secondhand smoke every other night at band practice since Sage insists he plays better when the garage is being hotboxed.

As I'm gazing out the window, I suddenly notice something odd on the sidewalk below. A middle-aged bald guy with a beer gut and a gnarly looking scar on his jawline is walking his dog. He pauses in front of the Gregory's home and stares at the house. He could easily be gawking at the freshly hung twinkling lights and decorations, but his attention lingers on Ayden's bedroom window for far too long in my opinion. Then the man scurries away, tugging his dog along with him.

I make a mental note to mention the guy to my mother when I see her later tonight. I'm sure he is just some random dude being a gawker. But, with how worried everyone's been lately and with the police telling Lila to keep a closer eye on Ayden, it feels imperative to at least bring it up.

After the guy vanishes, I turn from the window and collect my phone from my dresser to text Ayden.

Me: U about ready to get this funfest on the road?

Ayden: Yeah, I'll be over in like ten. I'm in the middle of something.

Even though we're already running late, I don't push him to hurry his butt up. I slip on my leather jacket, tuck my phone into the pocket, and pop in my earbuds. I crank up a little "For You, And Your Denial" by Yellowcard and flop down on my bed with my notebook I jot lyrics in.

Despite how collected I am around Ayden, my composure crumbles and splatters across the pages the moment I pick up a pen. Penning lyrics has become my outlet and my sanctuary, a time when I feel okay not being so cheery and smiley.

Can you hear me crying?
Silent agony that will completely vanish.
A scorch in my heart,
Singeing into embers.
My veins char to ash.
Hardly a flicker of fire left
To ignite life into me again.
Eventually the cold settles
Through my skin into my bones.
The embers drown with mourning,
Stealing the last breath of air.
And that silent cry dies,
Takes its final breath of air,
Caves to the chill.
Nothing is left, left, left.
Fading, withering, dying.

I pull the pen away. Okay, maybe my parents do need

to worry about my mind.

I scratch my head as I reread my gloomy and slightly morbid lyrics. I don't know why, but I kind of like them.

Feeling satisfied, I tuck my notebook away then turn to the window again to check on Ayden. His bedroom light is off, so he has to be heading over. Down in driveway, Uncle Ethan and my dad are sawing off the bottom of a tree. Kale and Fiona, Uncle Ethan and Aunt Lila's other adopted children, are with them, gathering the stray tree branches and carrying them inside the Gregory's home to make wreaths like they do every year.

Ayden is nowhere in sight.

Me: Dude, where are you at?

He doesn't respond.

About a minute later, I spot him hurrying up the sidewalk from the direction of the main road with the hood pulled over his head. Instead of cutting across the front lawn, he hunkers down behind the neighbor's fence then climbs over it into his side of the yard. With his back pressed against his house, he inches toward the front door like a ninja, clearly trying to go unnoticed. But why? And where was he for the last ten minutes or so?

To make the situation sketchier, the instant he slips into the house, he texts me back.

Ayden: Just got out of the shower. Be over in a couple.

"That little liar," I utter under my breath.

I wait near the window until he exits through the back-door. He waves to my dad and his, then jogs around the fence to my yard. Like always, he knocks on the door before walking in.

My dad turns to him from the driveway and hollers, "Ayden, you can just go in!"

I pull my earbuds out and wait for him to walk into my bedroom. When he strolls in with damp hair, as if he actually took a shower, my jaw ticks with irritation.

"All right, buddy." I stare him down hard. "What are you keeping from me?"

He averts his gaze to the floor, ruffling his hair into place. "What are you talking about? I've been at my house." He scratches at the corner of his eye, and I notice a phone number on the back of his hand.

What the hell has he been up to tonight? And, better yet, who has he been with?

And why is he lying to me?

27

Chapter 2

Ayden

She has a very un-Lyric like expression on her face when I walk into her bedroom. She's upset, maybe with me. After a week of being extra nice and agreeable, her determined attitude instantly throws me off. Then she bluntly calls me out on keeping something from her, and I know it's only a matter of time before I spill my secret, because upsetting her will quickly wear me down.

"What do you mean?" I mess with my damp hair. Since I texted Lyric that I'd just gotten out of the shower, I actually had to get it wet in the bathroom sink before I headed over. I ended up getting the collar of my shirt wet in the process, making the back of my neck cold.

"Don't 'what do you mean' me, looking all innocent." She strides across the room then pokes me in the chest. "You know, usually I'm cool with you not telling me stuff, but when I see you creeping up to your house all ninja style then lying to me about where you were, telling me you were taking a shower," she rolls her eyes, "that's when I

28

start pressing for info. So, tell me, where'd you sneak off to tonight?"

"I…" I trail off as she elevates her brows at me.

For the last two weeks, I've spent night after night wondering if my brother's death was a murder caused by the people who held my siblings and me captive three years ago. His body had been found near the house we'd been held hostage. If it was the same people, I worry they'll eventually try to kill my younger sister and me. My sister who I wish I could see again, if for nothing other than to know she's safe.

Fear, toxic fear,
driving me insane.
Flooding me with rage.
Fear, toxic fear,
I wish you'd just disappear.
Leave me alone.
Get the hell out of here.
But I know you'll never go away,
let me breathe again,
until I know my sister's safe.
Until I know the demon has paid.

On day five of barely sleeping at all, I decided I'd had it with the constant worry and started searching around on the Internet. I'd stumbled across a hacker and met the guy tonight in the park near my neighborhood because he refused to have business meetings over the phone or computer. Not the smartest thing to do on my part, but I'm getting desperate.

Of course when I met him, my worries of whether he was a serial killer or not dissolved. Rebel Tonic—an online name—is a gangly guy younger than me. If he tried anything, I could have taken him if I had to.

He insisted he can find my sister's whereabouts by hacking into social service's records. His fee is more than I have stashed away, so I'm trying to figure out where to come up with the money, and if I can even trust him not to screw me over.

"I can't tell you." I offer Lyric an apologetic look, wordlessly begging her to please be understanding like she normally is.

Her mouth plummets to a hurt frown. "Why not? You know I'll keep whatever you tell me a secret."

"I know you will… that's not the problem." I tangle our fingers together and guide her to the bed, drawing her with me as I sit down. "Trust me, it's not because I don't want to tell you. I just don't want to get you into trouble if I get caught. It's better if you don't know what I'm up to just in case our parents find out... It's better if you're in the dark, at least for now."

"You're worrying me. Is it...?" She bites on her bottom lip. "You're not doing anything illegal or dangerous are you? Like... drugs?"

"What! Drugs... do you really think that about me?"

She looks shamefaced. "No, but... I heard Aunt Lila whispering it to my mom the other day. I think she's worried about you because you seem so... depressed." Caution creeps into Lyric's voice, probably worried she's crossing a line with the remark about my emotions.

"I know she is." And I feel bad. The last thing I ever want is for anyone to worry about me. I wish I could be happier so my family could relax, but I feel so depressed all the time. "I'm not doing drugs, though."

"I figured you weren't, but I had to ask." She intently studies me with her green eyes then her bottom lip juts out into a full-on pout. "You really won't tell me what's going on?"

31

It's difficult to tell her no when she looks as adorable as she does right now. I just want to kiss her lip, suck it in my mouth...

"Lyric... I..." Her pout deepens, and I sigh. "You know, when I first met you, I thought you used to do the whole pouting thing unintentionally." I tuck a strand of her long, blond hair behind her ear, highly aware of how badly my fingers tremble and the way her breath hitches in her throat. "But now I'm starting to wonder if you know exactly what you're doing."

"So does it work?" she asks, hopeful. "Does it mean you'll tell me where you were?"

"Not yet... but soon... maybe. If I feel like it's safe to."

"How soon is soon, though? Because you've got me really, really worried about you, to the point where it's hard to think about anything else."

"I don't want that. You don't need to put so much... effort into being my friend all the time, especially with how much of a burden I've been lately."

"Like I could simply just quit." She shakes her head and her smile brightens. "You're my favorite person. And it's hard to just stop thinking about my favorite person. But

and jotted his phone number on my hand with every intention of transferring the digits to paper when I got home, but then I got sidetracked with rushing over here and forgot to wash the number off.

"God, I just made things super awkward, didn't I?" Lyric mutters with a disheartened sigh. "After being like the coolest person ever, I've resorted to an awkward, unsure girl." She stretches her fingers out and focus on her hands. "Can we pretend I didn't just act like a jealous weirdo? It could be your early birthday present to me."

My heart thuds deafeningly from inside my chest as I hook a finger under her chin and tip her face up. "You're not acting like a jealous weirdo. You're acting like a normal person. I'm the one who's been the weirdo, shutting you out like I have. It's not fair." My heart rate quickens even more as she wets her lips with her tongue and briefly glances at my mouth.

God, if I could just kiss her without freaking out...

I'd kiss her all the time.

"So, just to be clear," my voice wobbles embarrassingly, "I'd never go on a date with someone else. I don't want to date at all. I mean, I do want to date, but I just can't yet. I don't think so, anyway." I clear my throat. Nothing I'm saying is coming out right. "Okay, let me try that again. I don't want to go out on a date with anyone other than you. I just don't think I can handle dating right now." I roll my eyes at myself. Man, I am the least smooth person ever. "See, now I'm the one who just made things awkward."

"You didn't make things awkward." She searches my eyes, her own sparkling, a sign that my cheery Lyric is about to emerge. "So, my dad had a band cancel for his opening."

Her abrupt subject change throws me off, but I latch on to her offering. It's one of the reasons I love her so much...

Love her?

I shake my head at my thoughts, and Lyric's face twists with perplexity.

No, I like her.

A lot.

I don't even know what love is.

I can't.

Can I?

"Did you offer up our help?" I absentmindedly twist a strand of her hair around my finger, shutting down my thoughts before I freak out.

"Well, duh." She rolls her eyes then grins. "Of course I did."

With each soft tug of her hair, her eyelids flutter and her lips part.

And with each eyelid flutter and lip part, my pulse throbs.

I don't stop.

I don't want to stop until it becomes too much for me.

"And what'd he say?" My voice is surprisingly husky.

She moans, and that's when I finally lose it, when I know I've pushed my emotions too far. Images start to creep into my mind; a brush of hair and caresses of finger-tips I don't want touching me.

I untangle my fingers from her hair as a breath falters from my lips.

Lyric frowns disappointedly but doesn't say anything. "The same old, same old." She makes a flapping motion with her hand as she pulls a face, pretending to mimic her dad. "He yammered about my mental stability, said I need-ed more stage preparation, and that *he* needed more preparation for his daughter to freakin' rock the socks off a bunch of people."

My lips twitch in amusement. "And what did you tell

him?"

"I told him we rocked, and if he heard us, he'd beg us to be in his lineup. I gave him something to really think about." She winks at me. "Now, we should probably go practice for when he asks to see us play." She laces her fingers through mine, rises from the bed, and then pulls me up with her.

"You really think he's going to?" I question as we head for the door.

"Oh, yeah. I could see it in his eyes." She points at her own. "He was totally wondering just how talented his daughter really is. In fact, I bet by tomorrow he'll be asking to hear us play."

"You really think we're ready, though?" I ask as we descend the stairway toward the main floor of the two-story home. "I mean, we don't even have a band name yet."

"I have a few ideas for that." She peers over her shoulder at me, her eyes sparkling mischievously. "Have a little faith in me and my awesomeness, would you?"

"I have a ton of faith in you and your awesomeness. It's the rest of the band I'm worried about."

She squeezes my hand reassuringly. "We're all doing

well. Granted, Nolan's a little less motivated than you, Sage, and me. Do you ever get the feeling that his interest in the music industry is solely based on getting laid?"

"I've thought that a lot," I reply as we enter the dimly lit kitchen that smells like vanilla with a hint of cleaner.

A plate of cookies Lila sent over this morning is on the countertop along with a stack of neon pink flyers for the opening of Infinite Bliss, Lyric's dad's new club.

"He's so old school," Lyric remarks as she picks up a flyer.

"He didn't do any other promoting?" I steal a cookie off the plate.

"No, he did after I made a suggestion that flyers don't work that well anymore." She drops the flyer back onto the stack. "See, he totally owes me." She grabs two cookies off the plate then steers us out the back door and to the driveway. "I just wish he'd realize that." She puts the cookies in her mouth so she can open the garage door without letting go of my hand.

The night sky is lit up by the moon and the countless stars and matches the illuminated neighborhood covered with Christmas lights and decorations. I've lived here for over a year and still can't get over how different it is from all the other homes I stayed at. So bright, cheery, welcoming. All the other homes were full of despair and were energy draining.

"Who is that?" Lyric suddenly asks.

I track her gaze to a man with a dog on a leash wearing a tracksuit. He's slowly walking down the sidewalk with his attention on my house, specifically focusing on the second story, right on my bedroom window.

"I don't know. He's probably just some neighbor wondering why we have a half-deflated Santa near the front door of the house."

My thoughts laugh at me, whisper another story, remind me that it was my neighbors who took me into their home and broke my brother as well as my sister and me.

Sharp objects, have you forgotten?

All those days forced into restraints.

All the blood spilled across the carpet.

The stench of rust hanging in the air.

Trust. Trust. Trust.

How can you still be so naïve?

Lyric looks at me with concern. "Yeah, I guess so … but he's not even looking at the front door. And I think I saw him earlier, too, and he looked like he was staring at your window."

I squint through the darkness to get a better look at him: middle-aged, going bald, a beer gut, and what looks like a scar on his jawline. For a brief moment, I pause, trying to connect the guy to my past. But my effort is worthless. The people who kidnapped me are buried in the darkest parts of my mind along with the memories of what they did to me.

"He looks like almost every other guy who lives on the street." My inner voice laughs at me again. "I'm sure it's nothing." Even I don't sound that convinced by my words, though.

"Maybe." Lyric sounds doubtful. "Ay, I don't want you to be upset with me for bringing it up, but... I was thinking about how those detectives said that maybe Aunt Lila and Uncle Ethan should keep an extra eye on you until they can figure out who was behind..." She anxiously waits for me to say something. When I don't, she tacks on, "Maybe we should mention something to them, just in case."

My eyes wander back to the man and I realize the he's looking right at us. I instantly stumble back into the shadows and pull Lyric with me. Then I position myself in front of Lyric to protect her from being seen.

"Do you think he can see us?" Lyric whispers, fisting the bottom of my shirt as she peers over my shoulder.

"Not now." My body convulses with spasms as her knuckles graze my lower back, but she doesn't appear to notice, too preoccupied by the man. "But I'm sure he did before we ducked back here."

I observe the man from around the corner of the garage. He continues to stare in our direction, before finally fixing his attention back on my house. Then with a jerk on the dog leash, he scurries down the sidewalk toward the end of the block and out of sight.

"That was weird." Lyric steps around me, the absence of her warmth leaving me oddly cold inside. "We should definitely mention it to Aunt Lila."

"Yeah, I guess we should. If you think so, anyway." When I face her, she scowls at me. "What?"

"Not you guess," she scolds. "You *will* tell her, or *I* will. I don't care if it's nothing. After … what happened, I'm not going to risk it, risk something happening to you."

"There's no use arguing with you, is there?"

41

"Nope. Not about this."

"All right. When we get home from band practice, I'll make sure to bring it up to Lila. Only for you, though. I'm not worried."

Liar, liar,

all the time.

Worry dances in your mind,

round and round,

a broken record.

A song stuck on repeat,

singing through veins

as you lie restlessly in bed.

Liar, liar,

all the time.

Always worrying they'll return,

and death will burn your skin again.

A few minutes later, when we're satisfied the man isn't going to return, we pile into Lyric's dad's 1969 Chevelle since the Challenger her dad bought her a little over a month ago is nowhere near ready to drive yet. Then we buckle up, turn on the radio, and Lyric slams the gas pedal down. The tires squeal as she backs down the driveway and onto the road.

"If you're not careful, one of these days, someone is going to call the cops on you about your driving," I tease as I relax back in the seat. Just being with her gives me a little bit of inner peace sometimes.

"If it happens, it happens." She cranks the wheel and fishtails the car onto the main road with an up-shift. "I mean, what are my parents going to do, get mad at me? My mother's gotten more tickets than I can count."

"True." I pick up the iPod from the dock and start browsing through the songs. "But they could—"

My phone vibrates from inside my pocket. I fish it out and swipe my finger over the screen to read the text message.

Lila: We need to talk about something important when you get home.

Me: Okay. What's it about?

I grow anxious that perhaps she found out I met with a hacker tonight. I haven't been punished very much by the Gregorys—I've tried to stay out of trouble as much as possible ever since they adopted me. I'm guessing with something as severe as illegal hacking, their relaxed approach at parenting would disappear.

43

Lila: I really just want to talk to you about it when you get home, not on the phone.

Me: Okay. I'll be home in a few hours. Can you at least tell me if I need to be worried?

Lila: No, no need to be worried.

I start to put my phone away when another text comes through.

Lila: I don't want you to worry all night, and knowing you, you will. It's about the police. They want to talk to you again about your brother. Please don't panic. I'm sure it's nothing.

I probably should respond to her message, at least to tell her I'm okay, but I can't think of what to say.

"Everything okay?" Lyric asks.

I concentrate on the song list again. "Yeah, of course."

She watches me instead of the road. "Who was that text from?"

"Lila. She just wanted to let me know she needs to talk to me about some stuff when I get home."

"Are you sure that's all she wanted?"

I nod, unable to look her in the eyes, knowing she'll see right through my lie.

Liar, liar, alone in the dark,

Hide the truth from your heart.

Lock your soul in a box.

Melt the key.

Set the box on fire.

And burn it into oblivion.

Let the ashes scatter the ground.

And never utter a sound.

Liar, liar, alone in the dark.

Lyric's chest rises and falls, as if she's struggling to breathe. "If you don't want to tell me, then that's fine. But just say so. Don't lie to me, please."

God, I'm the biggest asshole ever. I really am.

"The police want to talk to me." The words are difficult to say.

Her gaze glides to mine and her grip tightens on the wheel. "When do they want to talk to you? Tonight?"

I shake my head. "I don't think so, but Lila didn't say."

"Are you... Are you going to be okay? I mean, with talking to them."

"I don't know," I admit honestly. "I guess it depends on what they want to talk about. She said something about my brother, but I'm not sure if it's details about his death or my"—I swallow hard—"memories."

I think I already know for sure, though. Lila warned me the morning after we learned the news of my brother's death that the police may want my help in solving his murder by remembering what happened those weeks we spent with our captors. They believe if I can remember then maybe I can help identify them.

If that's what they want me to do... Well, I'm not sure I can handle it. I locked up the memories for a reason.

Dying flesh.

Ruptured heart.

Scars searing.

Flaming soul.

The touch of death

burns through my skin

and strikes at my bones.

Resuscitated and revived,

but not without sacrifice.

Close up my mind.

Forget what I saw.

What I heard.

What was done to me.

Remember and give up my soul.

Remember and submit to the pain.
Remember and wither away
into nothing.

Chapter 3

Lyric

It's been two days since I saw the strange man hanging out in front of Ayden's house, and I've been working on a drawing of the guy just in case it's needed. I don't know why, but I have the strangest feeling that the man was more than a just a neighbor passing by.

I've been having trouble sleeping the last couple of nights because of the man. Every time I close my eyes, I see him in the tracksuit with his dog. The twisted part is that his outfit sometimes transforms into a cloak and the dog shifts into a scythe, and I'm suddenly staring at the Grim Reaper.

No more horror movies for me for a while.

I debate whether or not to tell Ayden about my dream. In the past, he'd have found it amusing, but with everything going on, I doubt he would anymore. He still hasn't spoken to the police, nor does he know when he's going to, only that it'll be someday this week.

My family and all the Gregorys get together every year

to decorate the tree. After we're done, we'll all go over to my house and do the same thing. It's a strange little tradition that started during my first Christmas ever. Back then, though, Uncle Ethan and Aunt Lila hadn't adopted any children yet.

The massive tree Ayden and I picked out sits in the center of the Gregory's living room, trimmed and decorated with shiny silver and red balls that glimmer against the glow of the flames burning in the fireplace. Our parents are drinking eggnog in the kitchen and have already exceeded the tipsy point. Kale is eating popcorn and watching a Christmas movie while Fiona and Everson fight over who gets to put the star on the tree. Ayden and I sit in front of the computer doing a little research on his brother, ignoring the commotion going on.

He'd been so reluctant to even speak his brother's name that I was honestly surprised when he brought out the computer and said he wanted to look up stuff on him. But I wasn't about to ask him, too concerned I'd hit a nerve.

"I still don't get why we're looking this stuff up." I skim the paragraph on the computer screen. "Everything we've found out about your brother's case online is the same stuff the police have told you, right?"

"Yeah, but it seems like there's something else," Ayden mumbles, clicking the mouse on the Page Back arrow. "Like why he would even go so close to the house in the first place. It doesn't make any sense. Either he had to be kidnapped or his body was placed there for a reason." His voice cracks and he quickly clears it.

"Maybe he was just there revisiting his past... Did he have amnesia like you?" I rest my chin on his shoulder then immediately regret it when his muscles constrict.

"Not that I know of." Ayden taps a few keys. "But I didn't really see him after we were taken out of the house. We went straight to the hospital and were placed in the system not too long after."

"I'm sorry," I say, unsure why I feel the urge to apologize over something that has nothing to do with me.

"Sorry for what... it wasn't you're fault." He twists around, causing my chin to fall off his shoulder. "You shouldn't be apologizing for anything." He sketches a finger across my cheekbone.

An evanescent contact of skin to skin, but my body still flushes with heat. I lick my lips—I don't even know why. It's not like I'm about to kiss him in the living room in front of everyone.

His breath hitches in his throat. "Maybe we should—"

"Hey, it's my turn to put the star on the tree!" Fiona shouts, causing Ayden and I to blink. She plants her hands on her hips and glares at Everson. "You did it last year."

"Liar. You did it last year." Everson is holding the silvery star and reaches his arm up high. Fiona, being on the short side, jumps to get it, but misses it by at least a foot.

"Everson! Give me that star." Fiona moves to tackle Everson, and he dodges out of the way, laughing.

"Everson, you did put the star up last year," Ayden intervenes without looking away from me. "Give the star to Fiona."

Everson curses under his breath, shoves the star at Fiona, and stomps toward the doorway. "Whatever. She's too short anyway. She'll never get it up there."

"I will, too!" Fiona shouts after him, glancing from the star to the tip of the tree.

Ayden sighs, sets the computer down on the coffee table, and gets up from the sofa. "I'll go get you a stool," he tells Fiona. "Hang on."

After he leaves the room, Fiona reels around and faces

me with a haughty bob of her head. "So, what are you guys doing on the computer anyway? Just seeing what was up with Ayden's brother."

"Sort of."

"Well, you're not going to find anything on the computer," she says, chipping at a chunk of glitter on the base of the star. "Ayden's just going to have to remember."

Fiona's always been on the strange side, so I don't put too much thought into what she said. Instead, I reach across the sofa to steal a handful of popcorn from the bag on Kale's lap because I'm starving. With how tipsy the adults are, I'm guessing this night is going to end with takeout.

Kale's eyes instantly pop wide as I bump his leg on my way back to the side of the sofa.

"Whoops. Sorry." Curious to why he looks so terrified, I add, "You okay?"

He mutters a "yes" then tosses the bag onto the table and bolts out of the room like it's on fire.

"What was that about?" I stuff a few pieces of popcorn into my mouth.

Fiona shrugs. "He's just weird. Like Ayden. We all are really." She ravels a strand of her long hair around her finger as she gazes at the lights flashing on the tree. "I've always kind of wondered if Lila and Ethan did it on purpose."

"Did what on purpose?" Ayden inquires as he enters the room carrying a stool, along with two cans of soda.

"If Lila and Ethan purposefully adopted weirdoes." When Ayden places the stool in front of the tree, Fiona climbs on and stretches her arm toward the top. With a slight sway of her balance, she gets the star on then jumps backwards off the stool. "There. Look at how pretty it is." She admires the tree with a tip of her head.

Ayden returns to his place beside me, but doesn't pick his computer up. He hands one of the cans of soda to me then pops the tab on the other. "I think I'm getting tired of researching."

I tap my finger on top of the can before opening it up. "We can take a break, if that's what you need." I take a swig of soda, the fizz tickling my nose. "Anything you want to do in particular?"

"Want to go get your guitar?" he asks. "Then we can go upstairs and play for a little while."

I grin a goofy grin. "You know the way to my heart, Shy Boy." He really, really does.

I just wish I knew the way to his.

The next morning as I lie in bed, staring up at the ceiling as the sun begins to rise and warm up my room, I try to think of a good present to get Ayden, one that will cheer him up. Last Christmas I got him a signed album, but this year I want to get him something special. Something that will make him smile like he made me do yesterday when we'd spent over four hours last night jamming out to our favorite songs. It was a nice. I wish we could do that more often.

Knock. Knock. Knock.

"Lyric, I need to talk to you," my mother says through the door with another soft rap. "Are you decent?"

"Yeah, you can come in." I sit up in bed and stretch out my arms as she opens the door and enters.

She's sporting a holey pair of jeans and a faded black shirt splattered with neon pink, yellow, and green paint. Her auburn hair is pulled up, and her phone is clutched in her hand.

"Man, since when did you become an early bird? You know that's a sign of getting old," I joke, glancing at the clock on my nightstand.

She smiles tiredly. "I have to get some pieces done for the art show in a few weeks. And I've been up all night, so technically, that doesn't make me an early bird."

I plant my feet onto the floor. "Nope, it just makes you a crack-head."

She sighs her *oh Lyric* sigh.

"What?" I ask innocently. "Too early for jokes?"

"Or too late." She sighs again. "Lila and Ethan had to take Ayden to the police station this morning, so you're going to have to drive yourself to school today. And you need to take Kale with you."

"Oh." I fight back a frown. Ayden and I always ride to school together, and we stop by this little coffeehouse that has the best cappuccinos ever. Usually, he drives us in one of the Gregory's cars, although my parents occasionally allow me to borrow one of theirs when they're feeling particularly awesome. It's our morning ritual and I love it, just like I love seeing him. "Do you know when he'll be back? I mean, will he be at school at all today?"

"I'm not sure. They weren't sure how long they'd be there."

"Do you know why they're there? What they wanted to talk to Ayden about?"

"I didn't ask." She sits down on the bed beside me. "I figure it's really none of my business unless Lila wants to talk to me about it." Her stern expression presses that it should be none of my business, either, unless Ayden wants to talk about it with me.

Sometimes I feel like she knows more about Ayden than I do. I've overheard Lila whispering stuff about his past to my mom. I'm not sure what since they either shoo me away or leave the room themselves when they noticed I'm listening, and prying it out of my mother was impossible.

"I'm his best friend." I pick at a loose string on the hem of my pajama shorts. "He should want to talk to me about it, but he never seems to want to."

She pats my leg. "Unfortunately that's not how it always works. Sometimes even best friends need to keep stuff from each other. At least until they're ready to talk about it."

"Did you keep stuff from Dad? I mean, back when you were best friends."

Traces of remorse haunt her eyes. "There was a lot of stuff I didn't tell him. I kept more from him than I wish I would have."

I hug my knee to my chest. "Then why did you do it?"

She shrugs, uncomfortable. "I was afraid of what I would feel if I said stuff aloud. Afraid that your dad wouldn't love me anymore if I told him everything about me."

I rest my chin on my knee. "Just what kind of secrets did you have, Mom? You sound super sketchy right now."

She shrugs again and her eyes well up. "It doesn't really matter anymore. What's in the past is in the past." Sucking back the tears, she stands up. "You can drive my car to school if you want to, but you'll have to gas it up." She starts to leave, dabbing her eyes with her fingertips.

"Mom, wait." I spring from the bed and hurry over to her. "I'm not sure if I need to tell you this, but it kind of feels like I should, since I'm worried Ayden himself might not tell Lila or Ethan."

I quickly tell her about the guy standing outside the house, giving her the details of what he looked like, and giving her the sketch I drew of guy the night I first saw him. I omit that Ayden snuck out for a while, not wanting to get him in trouble. He still hasn't confessed what he was doing and I've given up on trying to get the information out of him. For now anyway.

"I'm glad you told me," my mother says when I'm finished. "I'll make sure to mention it to Lila. She'll want to know about it."

"You don't think he's bad, do you?" I gather my hair into my hand and fasten it into a ponytail with an elastic from my dresser. "Like maybe one of those people the police are looking for?"

"I doubt it." But concern masks her face. "But it's better to be safe than sorry." She glances down at the phone in her hand. "You should get ready for school; otherwise, you're going to be late." She walks out of my room and closes the door behind her, leaving me to stew in my own worry.

I decide to text Ayden to make sure he's okay; something short and simple, knowing that he's probably stressed out from being at the police station.

Me: Hey! If u need anything, give me a holler.

Then I put my phone down and get ready for school, waiting for him to respond and trying not to stress out when he doesn't.

Chapter 4

Lyric

Three hours and one silent ride to school with Kale later, Ayden still hasn't given me a holler, which should be a good thing, right? Means the visit with the police went okay?

Doubt resides in the back of my mind, though. Knowing Ayden, his silence could mean he's shutting down. Like my mother told me this morning, even best friends keep secrets from each other.

While I attempt to remain understanding, it still makes me sad. I barely know what's going on with him at the moment. If he's hurting while dealing with his brother's death, and what on earth he was doing when he snuck out of his house the other night.

"Earth to Lyric. Have you heard anything I've said at all?" Sage waves his hand in front of my face, interrupting my thoughts.

Startled, I jerk back in surprise and chuck the pencil in my hand. Our desks are facing each other, so the pencil ends up zipping by his head, missing his eye by an inch. Thankfully, we're in fourth period English, and the teacher, Ms. Reltingly, loves doing group projects, so most of my classmates are distracted and don't notice my crazy ninja reflex reaction.

Sage, of course, does since he's the one who caused it.

He cautiously raises his hands in front of him and leans back in his seat. "Jesus, Lyric. You don't need to get all crazy and try to stab my eye out." He leans over his desk, scoops up my pencil, and flips it through his fingers like a baton before handing it to me.

"Sorry." I check the time on the wall clock. *Holy shit! Lunch is in ten minutes.* "How long have I been zoned out?"

Sage shrugs as he flips a page in his textbook. "For about twenty minutes."

I casually glimpse around at the rest of the class; everyone is partnered up and working on the assignment. "Dude, I suck. I'm like the worst partner ever."

Sage fiddles with a silver barbell in his brow. "It's just class, no biggie." He releases his piercing and starts doodling skulls on the top of his notebook. "Do you want to talk about what's bothering you, though?"

I peek at the page he's on and turn to the same one. "Who said anything was bothering me?"

His brow cocks. "Lyric, you've been staring at the wall for the last twenty minutes and haven't said a word. Something definitely has to be wrong for you to remain that quiet."

I press my hand to my heart, pretending to be offended. "Are you saying there's no way I can just be quiet without something being wrong?" When he presses me with a look, I sigh. "Okay, you're right. But I promise it's nothing. I'm just waiting for Ayden to text me. That's all."

"Yeah, where the hell is he today? We were supposed to meet up before school to chat about something, but he totally blew me off and ignored my text, too."

"He had an appointment or something, and I think he must have forgotten his phone," I lie because I have no clue what to tell him. No one outside of the Gregorys and my own family knows what's going on with Ayden and the police. They don't even know about his brother's death.

"Yeah, if he's not texting you, then he's definitely forgotten his phone. What's going on with you two, anyway? You seem a little," he rubs his jawline, "offbeat lately."

"Whoa, nosy much?" I squirm, something I'm not a fan of doing. Usually, I'm comfortable in every situation.

"I'm just curious what's going on with you two ... for the band's sake." He shrugs and waits for me to answer his question. "You know, the last thing we need is some sort of lover's quarrel that causes us to split up."

I shoot him a dirty look. "Ayden and I aren't lovers."

"You sure about that? Because I can never tell with you two."

"Hmmm, let me think," I sarcastically say, thrumming my fingertip on my lip. "Well, there was that one time when we kissed under the bleachers and I nearly swooned on the floor. It was so magical." I roll my eyes. "What are we, gossiping girls?"

"Hate to break it to you, but you are a girl." He scans me over, his gaze remaining a little too long on my chest.

I cross my arms and decide to put him on the spot. "Okay, so why were you two meeting up before school? Because I'd really like to know for the band's sake. I mean, for all I know, you two could be having a bromance quarrel."

He stares at me blankly, clearly unimpressed. "You're

63

too clever for your own good, Lyric Scott." He tucks his pencil into the spiral of his notebook then leans back in his chair with a lazy grin on his face. "And I'm not telling you my secrets unless you tell me yours."

I scrunch my nose at him. "Well, this game isn't fun if you're not going to play."

"Sorry." He seems very unapologetic. "Besides, I don't want to talk about this with anyone until I chat with Ayden first."

"You're being very cryptic." I examine him intently. "You're not thinking about springing the band, are you? I know we haven't gotten any gigs yet and everything, but working my magic takes time."

"I know it does." He reaches into his pocket for his phone. "And it's not that. Trust me, I'm way too comfortable with you guys to ever start over with a new band." He reads something on the screen of his phone then smiles. "Well, looks like our boy got his phone back."

"Ayden just texted you?" I lean over my desk to look at the screen of his phone, but Sage quickly presses it to his chest.

"Dude, that's private shit right there, Lyric." He stuffs his phone into the pocket of his blue hoodie. "I know you and Ayden don't have boundaries and everything, but seriously, you can't just read people's phones whenever you want."

"Sorry." I'm not, though. I'm actually really curious to read what's on his phone, more than I was before.

"It's cool." He shuts his book, giving up on us finishing the assignment. "We should probably finish the project up after band practice or something since we wasted so much class time."

"Sounds like a plan." I close my textbook and shove it into my bag.

For the next seven minutes, I mentally chant the lyrics of an angsty song I wrote during first period, trying to cool off and not get jealous over the fact that Ayden texted Sage before me.

Am I another obsession?
An aching in your brain?
Am I a complicated attraction?
Driving you insane?
Tell me why I can't get you out of my head!
What it is you've done to me?

Why do you drive me so fucking crazy!

Please, please, tell me

Something.

Anything.

That will help me think

Clearly agaaaaiiiin!!!!

By the time the bell rings, I've chillaxed a smidgeon. I enter the busy hallway and spot Ayden leaning against the lockers across from the classroom. He's texting on his phone with his head angled down so he doesn't see me right away.

Sliding the handle of my bag over my shoulder, I push people out of my way as I march up to him. "Hey, what's up, buddy?"

His head jerks up at the sound of my voice, and he almost drops his phone. "You scared the shit out of me." He presses his hand to his heart and his breathing turns ragged.

My lips tug upward. "Clearly."

"Hey, we'll talk at practice later!" Sage shouts to Ayden as he walks backwards down the hallway. "I seriously have something important to talk to you about, so no blowing me off again!"

Ayden holds a thumbs up in his direction as he finishes sending his text.

I scroll over his black jeans, red logo T-shirt, his soft lips, dark eyes, and inky black hair to make sure every inch of him is okay. The last thing I ever want to do is be angry with him if he's hurt or something. When every visible part of his body checks out okay, I place my hands on my hips. "So, what's up with texting Sage before me?"

He scratches at the scars on the back of his hand, a nervous habit of his. "I texted him because I wanted to talk to you in person. Not through a text. I wanted us to go have lunch so we can talk in private. I want to… well, try to tell you what happened today."

"Oh." I feel so silly and kind of douchey for being irritated. "Sorry. I feel like an ass now. And kind of childish. I was thinking you liked Sage more than me."

"That will never, ever be true." He reaches for my hand. "And I'm pretty sure you could never be an ass, even if you tried."

I hold up a finger. "That isn't true. I'm pretty sure your brother thinks I'm an ass."

His brows knit. "My brother…? Oh." He shakes his

67

head. Again, I feel like an asshole. He probably thought of his real brother, the one he just lost. "You mean Kale or Everson?"

"Kale." We start down the crowded hallway with our fingers linked together, like we have every day since Ayden entered my life. "I had to give him a ride to school this morning. I think the kid is totally terrified of me. He wouldn't say a word, and every time I said anything to him, he scowled at me."

Ayden snorts a laugh as he weaves us around a group of cheerleaders blocking the middle of the hallway.

"What's so funny, Shy Boy?" I tuck my elbows in as we squeeze by a group of jocks.

I find myself searching around for William in the midst of them, since he generally hangs with the athletes. Thankfully, he's nowhere to be seen.

Hopefully, it stays that way.

"It's nothing." Ayden's lips expand into an amused smile. It's been a while since I've seen that smile, so even though I have no idea what's causing it, I smile, too.

"Tell me what's so funny." I prod his side with my elbow. "Or else I'll tickle you until you pee your pants."

His muscles spasm, and I worry that I've crossed a line

again.

"I'd like to see you try." He flashes me a genuine smile, and I relax.

"I accept that challenge." I poke him in the ribs.

"Lyric," he chuckles, wrapping his arm around his midsection for protection. "I can't tell you. Kale would get pissed off at me."

"I wouldn't tell him that you told me. Jeez, who do you think I am? Maggie?"

As if she senses us talking about her, Maggie suddenly appears in front of us with her hands on her hips and determination in her eyes.

"The date for my New Year's Eve party has been changed," she says to me as Ayden and I slam to a halt in front of her. Then she grins in Ayden's direction and not so discreetly pushes her chest out. I love the girl to death, but she really needs to stop drawing guys in with her breasts. "It's going to be December thirtieth."

"How can you have a New Year's Eve party that's not on December thirty-first?" Ayden's smile fades. He's unfriendly and cold to a lot of people, except me. For some reason, I've always been good at bringing out his inner sunshine. "It makes no sense."

"It makes perfect sense." She tucks her elbows inward to push her cleavage even higher. "A party's a party, right?"

Ayden shrugs. "I guess. But technically your party is a New Year's Eve Eve party."

"Clever." Maggie smiles then her gaze flicks to me, as if seeking some sort of confirmation that I'm okay with her trying to show Ayden her goodies. I'm not okay with it. At all. But I'm not about to get angry with her since I haven't been that honest with what's been going on with Ayden and me.

She searches my eyes then her posture relaxes and her cleavage sinks back into her shirt. "But, as clever as that is, I'm still calling it my New Year's Eve party." She points a finger between the two of us. "A party that you two better show up to."

She reels around and shimmies her butt down the hallway, drawing in a lot of the male population around her. She instantly zeroes in on her next target, the varsity quarterback. Rolling her shoulders back, she approaches him with what she calls her "vixen swagger walk."

"Man, she knows how to work those bad boys, doesn't

she?" I mutter, peeking down at my own breasts.

I'm barely a B cup, not that I care. Big breasts aren't going to get me what I want in life, but I have wondered what it would be like to overly fill out my shirts.

"Work what?" Ayden glances confusedly at me.

I point back and forth between my breasts. "These bad boys."

Even after being around my constant unfiltered mouth, Ayden still blinks in shock.

"Trust me, you could work yours, too, and get way more attention than she does." His attention drops to my chest fleetingly then he looks away as his skin turns bright red.

My own skin warms as I recollect when he reached up my shirt and brushed his fingers across my nipple. The torrid sensations I felt that night were like nothing I've ever experienced before.

I wish you would do that again.

Touch me like that

In my car,

In my room,

In my bed.

Touch me, touch me everywhere.

Instead of touching, Ayden and I silently head down the hallway with the buzzing of voices flowing around us. His palm dampens in mine or maybe mine does in his... It's hard to tell. We're tense, sexually frustrated as Maggie would put it.

"I'll tell you what I know about Kale," he unexpectedly sputters, breaking the tension between us. "But only on one condition." He releases my hand to push the door open and moves aside to let me through.

"Okay, what's the condition?" I step outside into the cool winter air, and goose bumps sprout across my skin.

Ayden lets go of the door then promptly returns his hand to mine, as if the ten second break from our flesh touching nearly drove him to a panic attack. My body, although cold, warms inside.

"That you never, ever repeat to Kale what I'm about to tell you," Ayden says as we start down the sidewalk and through the people eating lunch around the front area of the school.

"Okay..." I stare up at him, squinting against the sunlight peeking through the cracks in the tree branches above our heads. "You've got me worried."

"It's not anything to worry about." He grows quiet, spacing off as we hike across the freshly cut grass toward the parking lot. "But it's private enough that I need you to pinkie swear on it."

My lips part in mock shock, and I cover my mouth with my hand. "Ayden Gregory, don't you trust me?"

He stares up at the sky, stifling a smile. Eventually, his amusement gets the better of him, and he ends up grinning from ear to ear. He stops in the middle of the grass and raises his free hand with his pinkie hitched.

"Wow, where's the trust, Shy Boy?" I give an exaggerated stomp of my foot then link my pinkie with his. "I promise that whatever you tell me will stay between us. But, just so you know, that's always the case."

"I know; I just need to make sure, for Kale's sake." He tightens his hold on my pinkie when I try to pull away. "Just like I need you to promise you'll go easy on him."

"Okay, I promise, even though I have no clue what you're talking about."

Satisfied, he frees my finger, and we start walking again.

"I think Kale might have a crush on you." He glances

at me from the corner of his eye. "I've actually thought it for a while."

"No way." I wave him off. "Kale's the kind of guy who will get a crush on someone equally as adorably nerdy as him. Someone who's in love with comic books and wears capes on non-Halloween days."

"Clearly, you don't understand how a guy's mind works."

"Hey, I do, too," I say, this time genuinely offended. "I'm totally running on the same brain waves." Ayden's brows elevate questioningly, and I playfully swat his arm. "You seriously just lost cool points for that move."

He shrugs, unbothered. "Sorry, but I'm glad you don't run on the same brain waves as me. It would be weird."

"Yeah, you're right." I pause, contemplating what he said. "He really has a crush on me?"

"It's just a guess, but as a guy who's had crushes on girls before, I'm guessing that his awkward silence thing he does whenever he's around you means that he likes you."

I've known Kale since Lila and Ethan adopted him a few years ago. He's like a little brother to me, which makes the situation kind of weird.

"You get awkwardly quiet around every girl we cross

paths with," I point out to Ayden after we climb into Lila's BMW. "Which, by your theory, would mean you have a crush on all of them, including Maggie."

"Yeah, but I'm a freak of nature." He turns the key in the ignition, and the engine grumbles to life.

"So am I. I make love declarations about every guy I cross paths with."

He shoves the shifter into reverse. "You haven't done that in a while."

I draw the seatbelt over my shoulder and strap myself in. "Ever since William." *And since you kissed me.*

He rotates in his seat to glance behind him, but when our gazes collide, he pauses.

"Have you seen him again?" he asks with hesitancy.

I shake my head. "Not since that last time. What about you?"

"I saw him in gym. He didn't say anything to me, but he did try to hit me in the face with a ball during dodge ball."

"What a dick," I grumble. "I'm so sorry for bringing you into this drama."

"It's just a ball, nothing like a fist. And you didn't

bring me into the drama. I chose to walk in it because I care about you." A faint smile rises at his lips, one that warms me from my head to my toes. "Did you know his nose is crooked now?"

I perk up. "Really?"

He nods, his eyes burning fiercely. "I wish I would have broken more, though."

"The nose is good." I sketch my fingertip down the brim of Ayden's nose. "You did well, Shy Boy."

We exchange a meaningful moment, and then he backs the car out of the parking spot and steers toward the road.

"So, are you going to tell me what happened this morning?" I ask as he drives down the road lined with fast food places and restaurants.

"Yeah… Let's go pick up some lunch and park up near the bridge." He flips on his blinker to make a turn. "I want to be able to talk to you privately about some stuff before we head to town, anyway."

"Head to town now?" I ask, and he nods. "What about class?"

We only have a thirty-minute lunch break, and we wasted ten minutes getting to the car. Driving to the city limits of San Diego takes about twenty minutes, give or take a half of an hour for traffic.

"We're skipping the rest of school."

My nerves bubble inside me. *What the heck is going on?* "Why?"

"Because..." He nibbles on his bottom lip, mulling over something. "We're... We're taking a self-defense class, instead."

"Why?"

"Because my parents and yours want us to be safe, to make sure we can protect ourselves if we need to."

I'm not sure what to make of that.

Protect us from what exactly?

Chapter 5
Ayden

Five hours earlier...

The visit with the police turns out to be exactly what I was dreading. To move the case forward, they want me to try a few sessions with an amnesia therapy specialist.

"If it turns out to be too much for him or shows no signs of working within the first few sessions, then we'd like to try a few more aggressive methods," a detective who goes by the name Rannali explains. "I know this might seem a little extreme, but—"

"A little extreme," Lila cuts him off, her tone razor sharp. "You're showing no sympathy for Ayden, who's been through enough already and just lost his brother."

"Sympathy isn't my priority," he replies straightforwardly—he has been that way the entire visit, "solving this case is a priority. We truly believe that if Ayden can remember those days he spent in the house, he could help us identify some of the suspects."

"But I thought you weren't positive it was the same people," Lila points out. "That maybe he was just in the same area by coincidence. You said a lot of homeless people migrated to that area because the vacant homes were good shelter."

"Right now, tracking down those people is the best lead we've got," he responds vaguely, appearing mildly annoyed by Lila's excessive questioning. "And right now, your son is the last known person alive who's seen what these people look like. It's becoming a priority that he moves forward in his therapy. I know some therapists who come highly recommended for these types of things."

Lila's expression simmered with rage. "You don't need to be so coldhearted about it. You're speaking about him like he's not even a person. Just a tool to help solve your case."

"Help solve his brother's murder," he pressed as he coolly reclined back in his seat. "Do you know anything at all about this group of people?" He reaches for a folder on a filing cabinet then straightens in the chair. Opening the folder on the desk, he removes a paper and places it in front of the Gregorys. "They call themselves soulless mileas or warriors. Worshippers of evil, the list of the horrendous crimes these people have committed goes on and on."

Soulless mileas.

Soulless mileas.

Soulless mileas.

The name screams repeatedly in my head, but the noise is minimal compared to my accelerating heart rate. In the folder is a letter written in sloppy handwriting that looks an awful lot like my sister's. When I lean forward to get a better look, the detective hastily shuts the folder. He's not quite quick enough to stop me from seeing the signature on the bottom, though.

Sadie Stephorson.

My sister.

Detective Rannali avoids eye contact with me, focusing on Lila and Ethan as if I don't even exist.

"Wait? I don't understand," Lila says perplexedly to Detective Rannali. "Why are you mentioning these people?"

"We believe that someone in this group is responsible for the kidnapping of your son three years ago." He pauses with a brief glance in my direction. "And that they might have played a part in Felix Stephorson's murder along with several others over the last decade. It would make sense with his body being found close to the home Ayden and his brother and sister were removed from."

I want to shout at him to tell me why on earth he has a letter from my sister in the folder.

"Why would he have been there, though?" I ask. "Did they kidnap him again?"

"There were no signs of kidnapping," the detective answers. "But we haven't ruled out that theory either. We also have a theory that maybe your brother was looking for the people himself."

My back straightens in the chair as an icy chill slithers up my spine. "Why would he do that? It would make no sense."

Ignoring me, he drones on until I can't take it anymore. I need to know what that letter was.

After a while, I lose my cool and snap, "What was that?"

All three of them jolt at the sound of my voice.

"What was what?" The detective feigns being clueless.

I aim a finger at the folder. "That letter in there … It looked like it was from my sister."

"What's in that file is confidential," is all he says.

I turn to Lila and Ethan for help, but they only look at me with pity. Then Lila gently pats my knee and directs her attention back to the paper, leaving me to stir in frustration.

Why would they have a note from her? Is it old? New? Did she have something to do with this? Are they using her to help solve the case, too? Or is there more to it?

Ethan clasps Lila's hand when her eyes start to water. "Honey, relax. Everything's going to be okay." He looks at me. "We'll get through this together."

I know right then that the police are going to make me try to remember, that I don't really have a choice in this, even though they say I do. Besides, if I don't go through with it, I'm willingly making a choice not to help solve my brother's murder.

My throat thickens and my lungs constrict.

Force the memories up.

Then what?

What will happen?

To you?

To the person they all knew?

To the person you are right now?

He'll be gone,

as the chains wrap around.

Bind you in.

Make your head spin.

You'll lose your mind.

Lose control of your life

Again.

I only speak again when we're back at home.

I unstrap my seatbelt and say, "I saw that letter, and I want to know what it says. Is my sister helping the police, too?"

Lila and Ethan trade a concerned look, and then Lila rotates in her seat.

"Ayden, there's some stuff we don't feel like you're ready to learn just yet," she explains to me.

I don't want to get angry, but I feel the emotion scorching under my skin.

Before I can react, though, Mrs. Scott comes barreling around the fence and over to the car. After a lot of hushed talking between her, Lila, and Ethan, they take me into the kitchen and inform me that Lyric told them about the guy staring at our house. Then they inform me that, for safety purposes, I'm going to take Lyric with me to a self-defense class this afternoon.

Even though I'm upset, I don't argue. The class will be a good thing. Lyric knowing how to protect herself will be a good thing, especially with guys like William walking around.

Honestly, I can't wait to pick Lyric up from school. I feel so frustrated and know she will settle me down. Even in the midst of my darkness, through a storm of pain, Lyric brings me calm.

Chapter 6

Ayden

The present...

Lyric spreads her sunshine across my gloom the moment we reunite. Even when I tell her about the police visit, omitting the letter about my sister for the moment, I feel more at ease. The comfort remains during the entire drive to the self-defense class, but then the reminder of why we're there to begin with creeps up on me.

"Wait, I'm not dressed for something like this," Lyric says after I park the car near the back of a small brick building located about fifteen miles south of our quaint neighborhood secluded in the burbs.

I shut off the engine and slide the keys out of the ignition. "You look perfect to me."

"I'm sure I do, but as for being able to move around, which I'm sure is required in this class, these," she flips her fingers against her jeans, "aren't going to cut it."

"Yeah, your mom figured you'd probably need a

change of clothes." I reach over the console to the backseat and grab a bag. "She sent you this."

Lyric takes the bag from me and unzips it. "Where did she even get these?" She holds up a pair of black yoga pants and a purple tank top made of some kind of stretchy fabric.

I tap the tag still stuck to the fabric. "She must have just bought them."

"Wow, they must have been preparing for this." She tears the tag off, drops it into the bag, and tosses the empty bag onto the backseat. When she turns around, she starts undoing the zipper of her jeans.

"What are you doing?" My panicked gaze darts between her jeans and her face.

"Getting changed." She unfastens the zipper, lifts her hips, and then tugs down on her pants.

"Right here in the car?" With a lot of effort, I manage to keep my eyes on her face, even though my instincts beg to look downward.

She shrugs, shimmying her hips out of her jeans. "It's just underwear, no biggie. I'm even wearing my boy-cut panties that cover up more than my swimsuit."

Her pants are so far down I can see those black boy-cut

panties along with her upper thighs. Her skin looks so soft, so touchable. My hands quiver just thinking about brushing my fingers over her legs.

She suddenly halts her torturously slow strip tease. "Wait, am I crossing one of those boundaries again? I never know sometimes."

To Lyric, changing in front of her best friend is probably on the same level as wearing a swimsuit, completely innocent. But her swimsuit doesn't have lace at the bottom or a tiny pink bow on the front.

God, I just want to touch her.

My breathing accelerates with my thoughts as I desperately try not to panic.

Lyric must sense my anxiety because she begins pulling her jeans back up.

"Do you want to go find a bathroom at a gas station so I can change?" she asks, inching the fabric back over her thighs.

There are probably locker rooms in the building where the class is. I should tell her that or just take her to a gas station. But even in the midst of my semi-panicking, I'm so turned on I can't bring myself to utter those words.

"No, you're fine." I rip my eyes off her body and dig my phone from my pocket to busy myself with something other than gawking at her. "Unless you really want me to."

"I'm good changing wherever," she replies hesitantly. "And you don't have to look at your phone if you don't want to. I'm comfortable with you, Ayden."

I believe her. She's made it pretty clear that she wants to be with me as more than a friend. Right now, I wish I wasn't completely fucked-up so I could have her that way.

Have her on the backseat.

Touching her everywhere.

Her warm body underneath me.

Flesh to flesh of blazing heat.

Drowning me in warmth.

Taste it.

Drown in it.

Beg for more.

Kiss her like my life depends on it.

Like the blood running through my veins.

Kiss her until the darkness fades.

Kiss her, kiss the hurt away.

"Ayden?"

My attention drifts back to Lyric. *Fuck.* She doesn't

have a shirt on. Her bra has the same lacy trim as her panties do, with a pink bow right between her breasts.

"Are you okay?" she asks, fiddling with the bow in the center "You've been zoning out."

"Huh?" I blink away from her chest. "Yeah, I'm fine."

"Are you sure?" She bites the tag off the shirt. "You seem really out of it. And I'm worried the visit with the police is," she lifts her arms to pull her shirt over her head, "messing with your head."

The visit with the police…

Where stuff happened…

Where I was reminded of my past…

My head becomes foggy…

She hasn't pulled the shirt over her bra, still struggling to get the super tight fabric over her chest.

"The police visit did mess with my head a little, but that's not what's making me so out of it right now. It's just … I mean, it's you … and … you changing in my car in front of me." My cheeks warm.

Her lips form an *O* as her gaze drops to the shirt stuck on top of her breasts.

"It's really distracting," I add, feeling like an idiot

when my skin burns hotter, "to see you like ... that."

Instead of tugging the shirt down to cover up, she leaves the fabric up and bites on her bottom lip. "Good distracting?"

Her bluntness shouldn't surprise me—this is Lyric— yet I am. I'm stupidly surprised to the point that I just gape at her. She stares back, thoroughly amused.

What I wouldn't give to be like Lyric.

So at ease with life.

So comfortable in my own skin.

I sneak another peek at her chest then face the steering wheel and open my texts, even though I have no messages. "Of course it's a good distraction. You're gorgeous." My voice is low and husky in a way it's never been before.

Lyric is breathing so ravenously I expect her to say something dramatic and sexual. She never utters a word, though. When I finally look up at her again, her shirt is on, and she's putting her hair up.

"You ready to get this show on the road?" she asks coolly.

I nod and open the door, the cool air sweeping in and swirling around the cab, adding fog to the already fogged up windows.

"Wait. What about you?" She points at my black jeans, T-shirt, and combat boots. "Aren't you going to change, too?"

"Into what? Tight yoga pants?" I crack a smile for the first time today, but it still takes a lot of effort.

"Hey, you might look good in them with that cute, little butt of yours." She extends her hand toward me to pinch my ass, but I jump out of the car. She hops out, too, laughing her ass off as she shuts the door. "You should have seen the look on your face. It was adorable."

"And what would you have done if I hadn't moved?"

She skips around the front of the car and snatches hold of my hand. "Um, totally copped a feel, and I'd have been damn proud of it."

I roll my tongue along my teeth as a massive grin threatens to reveal itself. There are times when I wish I could spend every waking hour with Lyric. I'd smile a hell of a lot more and be way less depressed.

"You're blushing," she teases, moving in front of me and walking backwards without releasing my hand. "It's cute."

"No, I'm not." A lie. My cheeks are blazing hotter than

the sun.

"Okay, if you say so." She turns back around and walks beside me, gazing up at the blue sky, musing over something.

"What are you thinking about?" I ask as we approach the back entrance of the building.

Her fingers wrap around the door handle. "Nothing." Her head tilts to the side and I can see the wheels turning in her head. "It's just that..." Without warning, she reaches around and pinches my ass.

"Shit." I skitter back, my fingers falling from hers.

"Ha! Don't pretend you didn't like that." She yanks the door open and scurries inside, laughing.

I did like it. And I didn't like. I'm conflicted. Confused. Dizzy. Sick.

There's been so much touching today.

So much happening...

So much going on...

So much stress...

I think it might have been too much...

Too overwhelming of a day...

Something's wrong. I gasp for air as I shove the door shut, remaining outside, hoping Lyric won't see me like this.

My chest compresses, suffocating me. My vision gets spotty, and my surroundings are growing blurry. My bones ache, feeling as though they're going to collapse.

A young mother with children,
dancing on her grave.
Every day a battle,
never to be saved.
She can barely keep her head,
let alone her children fed
as she battles the monster
living inside her,
pushing her deeper into insanity.
She hangs on the edge
about to tumble into an abyss,
never to see daylight again.
Her skin cracks apart.
Her heart bleeds and rots.
She doesn't want this.
She wants to be saved.
Taken away.
That's what they *promise her.*

Saviors of the dark,

with empty promises of tomorrow.

Give into us, and you'll feel no sorrow.

Pathetically, the mother surrenders,

gives up her children to feed the monster within her.

They *take the children,*

drag them into their tomb,

cuff them up so tightly,

so achingly

they can't even move.

The pain sears their souls.

But that's just the start

of an unthinkable torture

that will shatter the children apart.

First, they take a hammer

and bash in their bones.

Then comes the needles

that dig into their skin.

"Ayden, can you hear me? Oh, my God. Please look at me. Ayden..." Lyric trails off as my vision comes back into focus.

It takes me a moment or two to process where I am; sitting on the asphalt, hugging my knees to my chest, and gasping for air. Lyric is crouched in front of me. Her skin is pale and her eyes are wide in horror. My head is throbbing as adrenaline pounds through my body. The worst part of the situation is the tears falling out of my eyes.

Crying for myself.

For my brother.

For my sister.

Crying because I almost saw the capturers' faces. And I don't want to see their faces, don't want to remember.

"I'm sorry." I quickly wipe my eyes with the back of my hand. *I can't believe I just cried in front of Lyric again.*

"Sorry for what?" She cups my cheek in her hand and tenderly smoothes her thumb across my skin.

"For freaking out in front of you." I put my hands on the ground to stand, but my legs wobble, weak like me.

Lyric places a hand on my arm and gently guides me back down to the ground. "You shouldn't stand up yet," she insists. "You were breathing pretty hard before you fell."

"Fell?"

She slides her hand up my arm to my shoulder then along my neck all the way up to my head. "Can't you re-member what happened?" She softly combs her fingers through my hair as she studies me.

"No. I can only remember getting ready to walk inside. That's it." I rack my brain for what happened.

Lyric opened the door to walk inside. Then she pinched my ass for fun. The contact broke something inside my head, something I thought I'd locked away to be forgotten. Add that to the stress of the police visit, and I lost it, completely crumbled. It's been a while since a blackout has happened, the last time being at the party where William assaulted Lyric.

"You're shaking," she whispers, scanning over every inch of my body. "Oh, Ayden. I'm sorry. I shouldn't have touched you like that. I set something off, didn't I?"

I shake my head, not wanting her to feel responsible for my mental instability. "It wasn't you. I honestly don't know what happened to me. I just sort of zoned out and sank to the ground."

"I think I should take you home." She stands to her feet then offers me her hands.

"No, you need to take the class." When I set my hands in hers, she helps me up.

The world spins around me as I get my feet under me. The blood rushes from my head, and I stagger around as I try to get my balance.

"I'll take another class later or find another way to learn some defensive skills." She slips a hand around my back and steers me toward the car.

"I didn't hurt my legs," I say, forcing a confident tone as my stomach churns. "I can walk."

Her grip only tightens. "I don't care. I don't want to risk you collapsing again."

Tired, I relax against her. Her warmth and scent brings comfort. Safe and cared about—that's what I feel whenever I'm with her. I'm lucky I have her—have this. I just wish I knew my sister had someone who made her feel safe and cared for, that she is okay. That the letter to the police was just her helping with the case, nothing more.

When we reach the passenger side of the car, Lyric moves her arm away to open the door then motions for me to get in. "I'm driving. You look too sick right now to be behind the wheel."

"What about your car?"

"When my dad gets home, I'll have him drive me to the school so I can pick it up. You shouldn't be driving right now."

I hand over the keys then duck inside. Lyric shuts the door and climbs into the driver's seat. I stare at the back of my hand as she revs up the engine. A lot of people think the scars on my skin are cat scratches, but they're from fingernails.

Put there by blood red fingernails.

A quiet humming builds in my skull, and my skin feels charred. I rest my head against the cool glass of the window as Lyric pulls out onto the freeway. I concentrate on breathing. Breathing, I can handle. Breathing is easy. Deep breaths, in and out.

We make the thirty-minute drive listening to Rise Against. My nerves settle the closer we get to home. But Lyric seems to grow more restless. By the time she parks the car in front of the garage, she's practically bouncing in her seat.

"Do you want me to come in with you so I can help you tell Aunt Lila and Uncle Ethan what happened, since you can't remember?" she asks as she silences the engine.

I shake my head. "I'll be fine. This has happened a couple of times, so they sort of know the drill by now." On-ly partially a lie. They know about my panic attacks, but the one I just had was more than that. It caused me to re-

Raveling You

member why tiny scars dot my legs and why two of my toes are crooked. Pins and hammers were used to inflict injuries on me.

I'm remembering.

Please don't let me remember.

I can't.

It hurts too much,

Will break me more.

And I need to be whole for the moment

So I can take care of some stuff—

Find my sister and make sure she's okay.

Nodding, Lyric extends her hand to the door handle. The pain emitting from her eyes tears my heart apart.

I catch her arm to stop her from getting out. "Lyric, I'm so sorry."

She sucks in a sharp breath before peering over her shoulder at me. "For what?"

I clutch onto her in desperation. "For being a shitty best friend, for making you sad all the time."

She rotates in the seat, facing me. "You don't make me sad all the time." She leans over the console. "You make me happy, Shy Boy. More than anyone ever has."

99

"Then why are you crying?"

"Because you're hurting, and I hate seeing you hurting."

My head slumps forward as guilt crushes my chest. "I just wish I could be a better friend to you," I whisper, squeezing my eyes shut.

Her forehead touches mine, her warm breath dusting my cheeks. "You're the bestest of bestest of best friends."

I smile, but the movement aches. Being happy right now feels wrong and energy draining. "There you go, making up words again."

She chuckles. "Didn't I tell you once that I'm that awesome?"

"You did." I don't open my eyes. Just feel her breath, her heat, allow her strawberry scent to encompass me. I want to kiss her so bad. I want to press my lips to hers in a soft brush, a quick taste, before I get out of the car and deal with everything waiting for me.

Everything about her sends my body into a mad frenzy. I'm walking a dangerous line right now, pushing myself far enough that I'm starting to remember some of the details of what happened three years ago. But fuck it. The police are already going to force me to split open my mind and let my memories out.

Just one moment with her. That's all I want.

Without opening my eyes, I dip my mouth forward and brush my lips across hers. She sucks in a sharp breath then lets out a soft whimper that causes both our bodies to quiver. Her lips willingly part, and my tongue slips deep inside, swallowing the taste of her. She groans in response, her fingers finding my waist and gripping tightly.

I gasp from the contact and instantly feel the memories scorch, bright and vivid, like hot iron on my flesh.

"I should go inside," I whisper breathlessly after I break the kiss.

"Okay," she utters raspingly.

A moment ticks by where neither of us budge, then we simultaneously move apart. Lyric climbs out of the car and heads to her house while I hurry into mine, wishing I was going with her. Wishing I was just a normal guy who could hang out with his girlfriend without flipping out.

But I'm not. I'm scarred, broken, cracked apart, bleeding out, and I don't know how to make it stop, how to fix myself.

I need to try, though. I have to try to get my life together and fix myself. Starting with my sister. If I can find her and know she's out of harm's way, then maybe I can have some peace of mind. Maybe I'll have hope that getting better is possible. Maybe seeing the images of my past can be just that—my past.

Maybe I can be fixed.

Chapter 7

Lyric

I have never been so scared in all my life as when Ayden fell to the ground. Then he looked up at me with tears in his eyes, and I just about died. My beautiful, sweet friend was crying and in pain. Seeing him like that was heartbreaking.

After we part ways at our houses, I start to wonder what caused the meltdown. Could it have been stress from the police visit, the stress of them insisting he has to try to remember his past? I don't know for sure, since he still hasn't told me much about his past. With Ayden, everything is in the present, which is fine—I'm all about seizing the moment—but it makes me wonder exactly what kind of terrible things happened in his past.

Needing to take my mind off stuff, I track down my father in his office to bug him some more about his club opening.

"Knock, knock, knock," I say, rapping my knuckles on

the doorframe as I enter his office. The usually tidy room is a mess. Papers are scattered on his desk, records are strewn carelessly on the floor, and empty energy drinks overflow the trashcan. "Whoa, did a tornado blow through here or something? Or is this just what happens when you hit stress mode?"

"What?" He closes his laptop then blinks around at the room as if he's just noticing the mess. "Oh, that. Yeah, I haven't had time to clean up in a few days."

I raise my brows at the mess that is clearly from more than a few days. "Want me to clean up?"

He shakes his head as he stands up, rubbing his eyes and yawning. "Nah, I need to get up anyway. I've been sitting at the desk all day." He stretches out his legs and arms. "What are you up to? I thought you were supposed to be at a self-defense class or something."

"That didn't work out." I plop down in a chair in front of his desk.

He starts stacking some papers. "Why? What happened?"

I shrug, spinning around in the chair. "I'm not sure."

He pauses. "You're not sure, or you don't want to tell me?"

"Both," I say, and he looks at me funny.

"Lyric, you need to go to those classes. With everything going on with Ayden and what happened with William," his jaw tightens, "you need to know how to protect yourself."

"Technically, I did protect myself from William. I'm the one who got myself out of that room after kicking the crap out of his balls."

"I'd still feel better if you took the classes. Ayden needs to take them, too."

"I was planning on it—we both were—but … I think Ayden had a panic attack or something, and we had to come home."

"Really?" He doesn't seem all that shocked.

"Did you know he has them?"

"No, but I'm not surprised with the stressful life he's had." He picks up the stack of papers and sets them in the desk drawer. "Your mother used to have them when she was younger."

I stop spinning in the chair. "Really? Why have I never heard about this?"

He glides the drawer shut then moves to the trash bin

to clean up the cans. "Because she hasn't had them in a long time. And she doesn't really like to talk about it too much."

"Is that why you guys worry about my mental stability?"

He drops the can he's holding. "Why do you think we worry about that?"

I push up from the chair and scoop up the can he dropped. "Because I heard you guys talking about it once. That I was *too* happy." I chuck the can in the trash bin. "You guys seemed pretty convinced that was a bad thing."

He collects another can from the floor and crunches the metal. "You misunderstood us." He tosses the can into the trash. "Your mom ... she just worries."

I start gathering the records on the floor. "Over what?"

He sighs, scratching the side of his head. "You know about your grandmother, right? Your mom's mom?"

"I know she committed suicide, if that's what you're getting at. But only because Grandpa let it slip out in one of his stories, not because you two told me."

"Well, she was bipolar."

"And...?"

He sighs again then takes the records from me and

stacks them on the shelf. "Don't take this the wrong way, but sometimes, your grandmother would get in these moods. These really, upbeat, happy moods that almost seemed unnatural."

I study his uneasy demeanor and a theory develops. "Wait a minute. Do you guys think I'm bipolar?"

"No," he says quickly, tense and guilty. "That's not what I'm saying at all."

"Then why do you look so guilty?"

His stiff posture loosens. "Lyric Scott, we don't think you're bipolar. Yes, we had to worry since it can be heredi-tary, but that's it."

"Well, to stop your worry, I'll just be blunt with you. I'm overly happy because I've had a super good life and I'm happy. That's it." I head for the door to leave. "And just so you know, I do get sad sometimes. I just choose not to be mopey for very long because life's too short to waste my energy on being sad."

I exit the room, even though I haven't discussed our band playing for his opening yet. But I'd wanted to cheer up, not sink farther into a bummer mood.

I go up to my room and rock out on the violin for a

while, seeking comfort from music. The soft tunes and channeled energy soothe my restless soul. By the time I put the bow down, I feel content enough to jot some lyrics down.

I grab a pen and notebook then flop down on my bed.

Look at the stars, staring upon the souls.
Watching them wander. Little pieces of their own.
Lost in a sea of others. Drowning in pain.
But there are too many to hear all the silent cries.
So we keep drifting, drifting, drifting
As the stars keep shining, shining, shining.
Watching, watching, watching us all fade away.

I withdraw the pen from the paper. "Okay, I'm not sure if I love what I'm writing or am terrified of it."

I decide to give my hand a break from my head. I hide the pen and notebook under my pillow then sit up. Outside my window, the sunset paints the greying sky with hues of pink and golden orange. I still have a few hours until band practice. I could work on my homework, but I want to check up on Ayden first to make sure he's okay.

Grabbing my phone from my nightstand, I pad over to

the window and send him a text.

Me: How r u feeling?

While I'm waiting for a response, the Gregory's sedan backs out of the garage and down the driveway. I can't tell who's in there, but I wonder if Ayden is.

Ayden: Yeah, I'm fine. Just resting now.

Me: At your house?

Ayden: Yeah.

Me: By yourself?

Ayden: I'm with Kale. Lila and Ethan just took Fiona and Everson to soccer practice.

Me: Want some company? I'm super bored.

Ayden: Lila actually told me I couldn't have anyone over.

Me: But I'm not just anyone. I'm your best friend.

Ayden: Sorry.

Sorry? What is that? A brush off or something?

Before I can think about it too deeply, Ayden walks out of his house and hurries down the driveway toward the sidewalk. His hood is down, and he keeps peering around as if he's nervous. When his eyes land on my window, I duck for cover and peer over the windowsill.

He lied to me again, snuck out of the house again.

"That little liar," I mutter as he veers right toward the end of the block, the same direction he wandered up from the other night when he snuck out.

Even though it might be wrong, I make the choice to tail him, worried he might be in trouble. Worried he'll blackout again like he did earlier. More than that, I'm just generally worried about him.

I snatch my leather jacket from my bedpost then run downstairs and out the door. I slip on my jacket as I jog across my lawn and turn right when I reach the sidewalk. I can't see him anywhere, so I pick up the pace, sprinting to the end of the street. Glancing left then right, I finally spot him crossing the street in a hurry.

Hunching down, I race after him, zigzagging behind trees and parked cars, trying to stay out of sight as much as I can. I check left and right before I dash across the street and hunker down behind a chain link fence near the park as Ayden slips through the gate.

I count to five under my breath then stand up and peek over the fence, crossing my fingers, hoping he hasn't spotted me.

He's striding across the grass toward the playground.

No one is around, except a guy perched in the middle of the merry-go-round. As Ayden approaches him, the guy hops to the ground. They meet under an oak tree and start talking about something, their lips moving as they huddle together. Then Ayden sticks his hand into his pocket and retrieves a silver object out that looks like a knife.

Something snaps inside me. Worry, fear, anger—perhaps a mixture of all three. Without any forethought, I leave my hiding spot, march through the gates and toward Ayden and his friend.

The guy spots me first. He says something, and Ayden reels around. Shock crosses his face, and he quickly shoves the object back into his pocket.

"Oh, don't stop whatever you're doing on my account," I say to Ayden as I reach the two of them. Up close, I get a better look at the guy. Lanky and on the younger side, with squared framed glasses and a pen tucked in the front pocket of his plaid shirt, he looks kind of nerdy. "What's going on?" My gaze travels back and forth between the two of them

"That's none of your damn business, little girl," the scrawny guy states, crossing his arms and narrowing his eyes at me.

"Little girl?" I mimic his move, folding my arms. Then I arch a brow and stare him down until he squirms. "Look, I think we both know I could kick your ass, so there's no use trying to be all badass." I turn to Ayden who's all squirrely himself. "What's going on?" The only thing keeping me calm is that maybe he has a good reason for lying to me. "Why are you sneaking off," I nod my head at the other guy, "to meet him?"

Ayden gulps. "Lyric, you need to go home. You shouldn't be here."

"Ouch. That stings." I press my hand to my chest, noting that it actually does ache.

"I'm sorry, but you do." His eyes narrow. "Wait. How did you even find me?"

"I followed you here when I saw you leaving the house after you texted me, telling me you had to stay in," I say coldly, shocking both him and myself. I hardly ever get angry, but right now, frustration simmers under my skin. "I'm sorry for getting snippy, but I'm worried about you, and until I'm not worried about you, I'm not leaving."

"Look, I know this seems a little sketchy, but I'm keeping you out of the loop for a reason." With a glance at the guy, his fingers circle my arm, and he steers me toward the gate. "You need to leave before you get into trouble."

I dig my heels into the ground. "Are you in some kind of trouble? Is that what this is about? Because I can help you if you are. But you have to tell me what's going on or else I can't do anything for you."

"I'm not in trouble." He withdraws his hand from my arm then rakes his fingers through his hair. "I just don't want you involved in this. If you knew what I was doing, you wouldn't want to, either."

"Well, tell me and I'll let you know if you're right."

He blows out a breath, his hand falling to his side. "I'll tell you, but you have to promise that, as soon as I do, you'll leave."

I shake my head. "I'm not going to promise that."

We silently stare at each other while the wind howls and kicks dead leaves across the dry grass and around our feet.

"It's about my sister," he finally surrenders.

My heart misses a beat. I wasn't expecting that.

"What about your sister? Is she in trouble?"

"That's what I'm trying to find out." He peeks over at

the guy, who is texting on his phone, and then leans in and lowers his voice. "Today at the police station, I saw a letter in one of the files that was from my sister. When I asked the detective about it, he told me it wasn't any of my business."

"Did you tell Lila and Ethan?"

"Yeah, and they pretty much gave me the same attitude."

"You think they know what it is?" I ask, astounded. "That they're keeping stuff from you?"

"I'm not sure. I mean, I'd like to think they don't keep secrets from me, but there's been a couple of times I've overheard them whispering about me, and I have to wonder if maybe they know more about my past, this case, and my sister."

"But how would they know?" The wind picks up and blows strands of my hair around my face. "And why would they keep it from you? It makes no sense."

I suddenly remember something I overheard the night the police broke the news to Ayden about his brother. A short conversation between Lila and Ethan when they thought I was out of hearing range.

"Ayden, I think maybe I should tell you something I

heard Aunt Lila and Uncle Ethan talking about, but after you take care of whatever you're doing with that guy, because he's staring at us right now and looks really, really creepy."

Ayden tracks my gaze to the guy then inches toward me protectively when the guy shoots me a nasty look.

"Who is that guy, anyway?" I ask, plucking pieces of hair out of my mouth.

"On the Internet, he calls himself Rebel Tonic," Ayden says. "I don't know what his real name is."

"Rebel Tonic?" I question with a *really* look.

"He's supposed to be really good with computers," he tells me as if it explains everything. "Good at hacking, too."

I try piecing everything together. "Is that why you're meeting him here, to have him hack for you? And is that what you were doing the other night, meeting him then, too?"

He warily nods. "I want him to hack into social service's records and track down my sister. I met him the other night and have been trying to figure out if I wanted to risk it and how the hell I was going to come up with the money." He pauses, frustrated. "After seeing that letter, I have to do this, Lyric. I need to know she's okay." He looks at me, pleading for me to understand where he's coming from.

I'm glad I can't understand, at least in the same context as him. I've had a really good life and will never fully comprehend what it's like to go through what Ayden has. I remember how I used to envy him, because he's experienced life. Now I'm grateful for what I have.

"How much does it cost?"

He stuffs his hands into his pockets and kicks the tip of his boot against the grass. "The fee is a thousand dollars."

"A *thousand* dollars!" My eyes widen. "Where the heck did you get that kind of money?"

"I don't have it all. I've saved up six hundred from the times I helped Lila with her catering events. The other four hundred I was going to pay off with..." He pats his pocket.

I eye him suspiciously. "What's in there?"

"A knife that belonged to my brother. It's rusty, but the brand is pretty high quality. I'm honestly not even sure where he got it from."

Tears instantly prick in my eyes. Here Ayden is, doing something highly illegal, risking getting into trouble, giving up something that belonged to his deceased brother, and he does it so simply, so matter-of-factly.

"You need four hundred dollars, then?" I mentally count what I have stashed in my sock drawer. After my last record shopping spree, I'm guessing about four twenty-five, give or take ten bucks.

"I'm not taking your money, Lyric." He pushes me in the direction of the gate and points for me to go. "Just like I'm not letting you get involved in this."

"Tough shit for you, but I'm already involved." I stand my ground. "You're my best friend. I care about you. And I'd be a freaking jerk if I just bailed out now."

"You'll still be my friend if you bail. You'll always be my friend."

"No duh. That's the most obvious statement ever. But I'm still going to go get you four hundred bucks so you can pay that asshole over there and keep your brother's knife."

"Lyric, I—"

I conceal his mouth with my hand. "Ayden, it's just money. It means absolutely nothing compared to our friendship." I remove my hand from his lips. "Now, go tell Mr. Rebel Tonic," I roll my eyes, "that I'm running back to the house to get some cash and not to go anywhere."

I raise my pinkie to make him swear he'll wait for me. Once he does, I start to jog toward the exit of the park but stop near the gates.

"Ayden," I call out, and he turns toward me. *"We'll* find her, okay? You don't need to do this alone."

He mashes his lips together, nods once, and then heads back for Rebel Tonic.

I run like hell for my house before Ayden can back out on our pinkie promise.

By the time I return to the park with a ball of money in my pocket, I'm sweaty and breathless. Relief washes through me when I spot Ayden and Rebel Tonic hanging out on the merry-go-round. He hasn't left, which means Ayden didn't break his promise.

I approach them, reaching into my pocket for the money.

Ayden quickly jumps to his feet and blocks me from Rebel Tonic's view as I hand Ayden the cash.

"I'm going to pay you back every penny," he promises as he stares at the bills in his hand.

I wave him off. "Let's just get this guy paid and go home." He turns toward Rebel Tonic, but I capture his sleeve. "Are you sure you can trust him?"

He lifts his shoulders and shrugs. "I don't know, but it's the only idea I have."

I free his sleeve and Ayden gives Rebel Tonic my wad of cash along with a crumpled stack of his own. Rebel Tonic counts it out, and then a greedy grin forms on his acne-covered face.

"Fan-freaking-tastic," he says, balling up the bills and stuffing them into his jacket. "Give me like a week, and I should have the information for you."

"How are you going to contact me?" Ayden asks as Rebel Tonic backs toward the gate.

"By email," he tells him, pushing his glasses up the brim of his nose. "And don't try texting me on that phone number I gave you the other day. My mom took my phone away."

"His mom? How old is he?" I frown, doubtful that this ordeal is going to end well with Rebel Tonic. The only thing that stops me from chasing his skinny butt down and snatching the money back is the glimmer of hope in Ayden's eyes.

"I'm not sure," Ayden mutters with his eyes still fixed

on Rebel Tonic. "Maybe like fifteen?"

"As old as Kale?" Yeah, I highly doubt this is going to end well.

Ayden finally looks at me when Rebel Tonic disappears out the park gates. The sky has shifted to stardust, darkness blankets the land, and the streetlights have clicked on, highlighting the way home.

"So, what were you going to tell me about Lila and Ethan?" he asks.

I scuff my boot across the grass. "The night we heard the news about your brother, I overheard them talking about how they knew your brother getting … killed was a possibility, that the people were out there, and they could come for you guys or something like that."

He rubs his hand across his forehead. "I knew that, too. That it was a possibility."

"Oh," I say at the same time he adds, "But…"

"But what?" I press with interest.

"But I don't know. I'm starting to wonder if they know more about my sister, brother, and me than even I know."

Silence encases us.

"What are you going to do?" I finally ask, zipping my jacket up all the way to my chin.

"I don't know." He draws the zipper up his own jacket then glances up at the moon. "We should get going before Lila and Ethan get home and notice I'm gone."

"Were you supposed to leave the house?" I ask as we hike across the grass.

"Not after what happened today. At the class, I mean. Plus, they're worried about that guy we saw watching my house."

"Yeah, I'm sorry I told my mom about that. I just felt that, with everything going on, they should know."

"It's okay. I'm glad you did. I should have told them myself."

I twist a strand of my hair around my finger. "Ayden, do you think what happened today … Was that a panic attack?"

He's quiet before he answers. "I was remembering stuff."

My head whips in his direction. "*What?*"

He exhales. "It happens sometimes … when I'm stressed out … or when things happen that remind me of my past."

We arrive at the iron gate and veer down the sidewalk,

past the homes sparkling with Christmas lights, wreaths, inflatable globes, and even some with artificial snow.

"Was it the stress of today?" I scoot over as one of our neighbors strolls by, giving us a friendly wave.

"Yeah, kind of," Ayden replies, waving back.

"Kind of? Was it the letter from your sister?"

"Yes and no." When I stare at him, silently pressing for more, his shoulders slump. "I don't want to lie to you anymore."

"Then don't," I say frankly. "When I told you that you could tell me anything, I meant it."

He contemplates what I've said. "It was because of all the touching we've been doing." His voice is barely audible and crammed with apprehension.

"Oh." My shoulders sink along with my mouth. "I get it."

He abruptly slams to a halt, grabbing my arm and stopping me with him. "No, you don't get it." Panic floods his eyes. "I want to touch you. I think about it all the time… Have ever since that day in your dad's office when I…"

I can't see his cheeks, but I can picture how red they are, like every time he talks about something sexual.

"When you got turned on," I calmly finish for him.

On the inside, I'm a wreck.

All the way back then,

His heart danced for me,

Spun a longing for my soul

And sought the taste and feel of me.

All this time, all this time, all this time,

He wanted me.

He bobs his head up and down. "You're the first girl who ever made me feel that way."

"The first that's ever turned you on?" I ask, astonished.

I've often wondered how sexually experienced he is, if he's still a virgin. The first time I met him, he was wearing all black along with a leather collar, gauges in his ears, and he was sporting black nail polish. I assumed back then that, because of his rough appearance, he was experienced. Then I actually got to know him and discovered how much he hated being touched, and I questioned my initial assumption. I still don't know for sure, since he never offers to talk about his past.

"You're the first girl I've ever wanted to turn me on." He chokes up, his hand on my arm trembles, and his fingers dig into the fabric of my jacket. "It's not the first time I've ever been turned on… just the first time where I wasn't… being forced…" His voice cracks.

His comment rolls over me like a vicious wave. What he's trying to say without actually saying it. That he thinks he's been sexually abused.

The reality of how harsh his life has been knocks the wind out of me. Why hadn't I thought of this before? With the way he hates being touched.

"Ayden, I…" I'm speechless, unsure what to say to him and freaking terrified I'll say the wrong thing.

"I don't know if anything actually happened to me in that house. All I know is that, at fourteen-years-old, I went into that house feeling okay with being touched. But, when I came out of the house…" He skims a finger along my jawline. "Sometimes, something as simple as a handshake can make me feel like I'm going to throw up. But I'm working it, working on getting better," he whispers, sounding as if he's trying to convince himself more than me.

My lips part as I prepare to ask him how he's working on it, but then his lips come down on my mouth. I stumble back from the unexpected contact and grab onto him to stop from falling. My fingers grasp his shirt, and I end up pulling him back with me. Losing our balance, we slam against the fence, but our lips remain fused together, even when Ayden moans.

"I'm trying," he whispers through kisses. His tongue tangles with mine as his hands find my waist and he pulls me toward him in desperation. "I want to be able to kiss you like you deserve to be kissed."

I have no clue what he's talking about, because I am being kissed like I deserve.

This kiss, it makes my body pulsate.

Makes flames blaze under my skin.

Steals my breath from my lungs.

But it's not really stealing

When I'm giving the air to him.

Willingly giving him anything he wants.

Just say the word, Ayden, and it's yours.

My heart.

My soul.

Whatever you want.

"Ayden," I gasp into his mouth as his body starts to quiver, "it's okay. I'm fine with how things are. And I love our kisses."

He abruptly pulls away, his solid chest heaving as he struggles for oxygen. "No, it's not... okay... nothing is." He avoids looking at me, staring at the corner of the street. The Christmas lights reflect in his eyes, making it appear as if he's tearing up. "You deserve so much better than some guy who can't even touch you."

"You *can* touch me." I grab his hand, lace our fingers together, and pull him. I refuse to let him go. Ever. "See."

His gaze drops to our linked hands. "It's not the same as if you were with someone else who didn't have so many problems."

"Of course it's not." I swing our hands. "It's so much better."

His Adam's apple bobs up and down as he swallows hard. "You say that now, but you'll change your mind eventually."

"No, I won't. You leaving my life would crush my heart, and I refuse to let my heart get crushed."

"It may take forever for me to get over this. And it could get worse when I start seeing the therapist for my amnesia."

"I don't care." I stand firm, knowing that, through all my indecisiveness and sporadic choices, I do want Ayden. I decided that the moment he kissed me for the first time to try to erase the painful memory of my first kiss that William stole from me. "I want this ... want you."

His hand shakes in my hand, but he nods his head once. I'm not positive what the nod means. If he wants this—wants me, too. If he's giving us a shot. I'm hoping so, hoping what he says is true. Because what I've said is the truth.

He'll crush my heart if he leaves my life.

Will I live? Sure. I'm not going to become overdramatic and think I'll drop dead if Ayden decides he can't be with me. Will my life be destroyed? For a while maybe, but eventually, I'll get over it the best I can. But there will always be a scar on my heart connected to every memory of Ayden. And I'd rather not have a scar.

I'd rather just have him forever.

Chapter 8

Ayden

Over the next couple of days, things are a little awkward between Lyric and I after I confessed that I might have been sexually abused. But I think we're just confused where our relationship stands. Are we friends? Boyfriend and girlfriend? I have no idea. I'd like to believe, after the conversation we had the other night, that we're the latter. But we haven't really said anything to confirm it. We behave the same as we always do. Still holding hands. Joking. She makes me smile. I'll take whatever she'll give me. I'm not even sure I could take more if she offered it. I wish I could offer her more, though. I meant what I said that night I kissed her near the park. She deserves better than what I can give her.

I don't have too much time to overanalyze what's going on between us because my amnesia therapy sessions begin this week. I'd be lying if I didn't say that I'm absolutely frightened out of my goddamn mind.

It's late in the evening and I'm lying in a lounge chair inside my therapist's office. My arms are tensely over-lapped on my stomach and my heart is pounding like a freaking drum, thrashing against my chest.

"Now, Ayden," my therapist, Dr. Gardingdale leans forward in the chair and hovers over me. A string quartet flows around me and the ceiling light flickers about every two minutes or so. "I need to make sure you want to do this. Because the last thing I want is for anyone to push you into this. It could make your Severe Post Traumatic Amne-sia worse."

Inhale. Exhale. I nod, even though I don't. Want is too strong of a word. Am I going to do this? Yes. But only for my brother.

"Alright then. I'm going to record our session for the police to review." He relaxes in the chair and reaches be-hind him to press the on button of a recorder. He taps the top of a timer. "And I don't want to keep you under for too long."

He had explained when I first came in that this was a lot like hypnotherapy. I'd never tried it before but had watched someone get hypnotized at a fair.

I suck in a deep breath and nod, my nerves jarring. "Okay."

"Now close your eyes."

"Okay."

"And relax."

"Ok...ay."

"Do you hear that, Ayden," my sister says. "Cop sirens. We're saved."

Saved? Is it possible?

"It'll never be possible," a woman whispers. ""You'll never be saved. Because if you escape, we'll come back for you..."

I rub my eyes as I open them. Blinking against the inadequate lighting, I sit up. "Did it work?" I ask the doctor. "Did I say anything?"

His sympathy tells me all I need to know. "Unfortunately no, but did you remember anything different?"

"Just my sister saying we were saved." I drag my fingers along the scars on the back of my hand. "And a woman telling me we weren't ever going to be saved."

"Well, that's a tiny bit of progress then." He stops the timer. "I don't want you to immediately get discouraged that you only were able to remember a little. These things can take time."

He continues explaining the details of hypnotherapy while I zone out and focus on the short memory I did see. See might be a stretch. Heard is more like it. No one ever has faces in the faint memories that return to me. They're just blurs, shells of people and places that I pretend don't exist.

After the session, I return home in a sullen mood and feel exhausted. I go straight up to my room to relax and play the guitar until Lyric comes bounding into my room, sporting one of her heart-warming smiles.

"I have an idea," she singsongs as she bounces onto my bed.

"And what's that?" I pluck a few guitar strings.

"Even though it's Christmas Eve and we're supposed to exchange presents," she kneels in front of me, "I think we should wait."

"Wait? But you love, *love* opening presents."

"True, but I was thinking it might be fun to do it later when life is a bit more cheery." She situates beside me and tugs the hem of her dress down as she stretches out her legs. Her hair is up, her deliciously looking lips sheen with gloss, and her green eyes radiate enthusiasm. "And it could be like a weird little tradition we do. Instead of being cliché and exchanging them on Christmas Eve, like a ton of people are doing all around the world."

I ponder her offer. "All right, you have yourself a deal."

"Good." She grins. "Because I can't think of a damn thing to get you."

I shake my head, faintly smiling. "I knew there was an ulterior motive." I strum the strings of a song I've been working on.

"What's that tune you're playing?" Lyric wonders, sliding her legs up and facing me.

"Just a song that's been stuck in my head."

"I like it… it's pretty."

"Pretty isn't very rock n' roll."

"Neither are you." She slumps her head against the headboard. "You're sweet and sensitive and piercing free." She touches the tip of her finger to the corner of my eye, causing me to miss the next chord. "You have such long eyelashes… They're gorgeous."

"So let me get this straight." I set the guitar down on the foot of the bed and turn to her. "You tell me I'm not very rock n' roll and that I have gorgeous eyelashes. I'm not really sure how to take that."

"You should be happy," she insists, her gaze momentarily flicking onto my mouth. "Being rock n' roll in a band is cliché and your gorgeous eyelashes make your eyes stunning."

My cheeks flame. I'm blushing.

"You're cute." She swipes her finger down the brim of my nose. "I remember the first day of school how I held your hand. I felt so special that you were all mine."

My heart flutters like an upbeat song when she declares that she pretty much claimed me a year and a half ago. "You are special," I say, wishing I was brave enough to kiss her right now. But after therapy, the doctor had said to take it easy with anything severely emotional. Just being with Lyric sparks emotions to life. Good ones like happiness and longing.

I pick my guitar up while Lyric fluffs a pillow and lies down in my bed. She watches me play for a while, running her fingers through her hair.

"So, how did your therapy go today?" she finally dares to ask as I play a song.

I shrug. "Not too bad, but that's probably because nothing really happened."

"You didn't remember anything at all?"

Another pluck, another strum. "Maybe a little."

"Okay."

I know she wants to ask what I saw, but she seals her lips together, suppressing her questions.

"It was when the police found us." I cease playing. "It was the last time I saw my sister… and she seemed so happy that we were saved." His jawline tautens. "One of the women that was holding us there… she said we'd never be saved… she warned me she'd find us again." My fingernails enfold into my palms, biting my flesh. "What if that's what happened to my brother? What if they went back for him? What if it's only a matter of time before they come back for me?"

"Ayden, you're safe." When I try to look away from her, she captures my face between her hands. "You have a family who loves you—people who love you. Nothing is going to happen to you."

Life would be less complex if I could wholeheartedly believe her. But after my brother's death, I can't fully accept that nothing will happen to me.

I rest my forehead against hers and take a few shallow breaths as she slips her leg through mine and aligns our bodies.

"What do you want to do for the rest of the night?" she asks, playing with my hair.

"Can we just stay like this? Can we just pretend that everything is okay for a while?"

"Of course."

She wiggles around until we're both lying down face to face. She keeps her leg between my legs, her hand on my cheek, and her forehead against mine. We fit together so perfectly it's mind-boggling.

How is this possible?

To completely fit with someone.

Our bodies creating lyrics

Perfectly composing

As our hearts dance together.

Nothing makes sense.

Yet everything makes sense.

Perfect is so confusing.

A dizzy spell inside my head.

Thirsting for answers.

With nothing to drink.

Where do I go?

To find out who I am?

Chapter 9

Ayden

I try not to worry over the failed attempt of restoring my memories and instead concentrate on the band. It's not like that session was the only chance for me to remember. Plus, part of me is relieved the session didn't work. Relieved I didn't have to relive the hellish nightmare. But another part of me feels guilty, like I'm not doing all that I can to help track down my brother's killer.

A couple of days later, I'm sitting in Sage's garage with Lyric, listening to music, attempting to focus on chords, notes, and the strum of my fingers. It's still Christmas break. December thirtieth to be exact. Everywhere I look still screams, *the holidays aren't over yet! Cheer up! We're starting a new year!* On top of everything going on with therapy, I haven't heard anything back from Rebel Tonic yet and cheering up seems impossible when the possibility that he ripped me off gets higher.

Things remain pretty quiet for the first ten minutes or

so while we wait for Sage and Nolan to show up so we can get band practice started. They were supposed to be here fifteen minutes ago, but Sage texted me and said they were picking up pizza on their way back from a concert they went to over the weekend. He also still needs to chat with me about something. He's been texting me for about a week now, but has never gotten around to actually telling me what he needs to discuss. I'd probably worry about it a little bit more, but I've had other things on my mind.

"Self-defense class should be called kick-your-ass class. I'm so sore," Lyric says, massaging her shoulder. "I feel like such a wimp."

"That's because you are a wimp," I joke as I strum a few chords on my guitar.

She shifts on the sofa and lightly punches my arm. "Whatever. I could so kick your ass if I wanted to."

"I was holding back on you in class."

In class, I'd been Lyric's partner, which required a lot of touching and human contact. I didn't flip out too badly, so I felt pretty proud of myself. I kept reminding myself that it was important for Lyric to be able to learn to protect herself, and in order to learn, I had to be a good partner. After everything she's done for me, I owe her so much.

138

"I could so tell, too." She fiddles with the microphone cord. "You're such a softie when it comes to me."

God, if she knew how right she is.

How much I melt just from just a simple look from her.

A glance in my direction

Sends my pulse racing.

Her green eyes melt away

The chill always in my soul.

I'm liquefying into something else,

Someone I don't understand,

Someone different.

Someone not so handcuffed to my past?

I wish.

God, I wish, that were true.

That the stress of my life was coming to an end instead of just beginning.

She prods the tip of her boot against mine. "You are doing okay with that, right? I mean, with all the touching we did in class?"

I twist the tuning pegs on the top of the guitar handle. "I'm fine. I promise. You don't need to constantly worry about me."

"That will never happen, so get over it."

Quiet stretches between us as I work on tuning my guitar and Lyric gets up to mess with one of the amps. She's wearing a short black dress with red flowers on the bottom. Every time she bends over, she flashes me. I don't look away. I have tried too many times and realize how pointless it is to fight my attraction to her anymore.

"Oh, I thought of a name for our band." She stands up straight, tucks a strand of her hair behind her ear, and then her brows dip. "Wait. Were you just checking out my ass?"

I shrug, staring at my guitar. "Maybe."

She laughs as she plops down beside me. "I so just busted you."

"Well, I wouldn't call it busting me since you willingly stripped down in front of me in the car. I've seen pretty much everything already."

She teasingly bumps her shoulder into mine. "Are you trying to flirt with me right now, Shy Boy?"

"Maybe a little."

She sweeps my hair out of my face. "You're so adorable."

I restrain a smile. "You do realize guys don't like being called adorable, right?"

"Yeah, right. You totally love that I do. Love that I give you little nicknames that no one else gets. Admit it."

"No way am I giving you that much power over me."

She grins wickedly. "Oh, yes you will." She tickles my side and my pulse soars erratically. "Because you love giving me what I want."

"True," I easily admit.

Her lips part to speak, but the buzz of her phone interrupts her. She scoops it up from Sage's stool, reads the message, and frowns.

"Who is it?" I set my guitar down on the floor.

"My dad." She texts something back then sets the phone down on the cushion next to her. "He was wondering where I was, like he doesn't know. I'm at the same place I am every Friday night."

"Are you two still fighting over the club thing?"

"That and the fact that he and my mom think I'm bipolar."

"I'm sure they don't really think you are. They just worry about you."

"Yeah, but instead of whispering about it behind my back, they should have told me." She reclines back on the sofa. "All my life, I've been taught to just say things how they are, not to hold things in or keep secrets. I was taught to be honest even when it's hard. They should be the same way with me."

"I know. I'm not saying what they did wasn't wrong." I relax beside her. "But don't be mad at them forever, especially when they care so much about you."

"I won't, at least over the bipolar thing. The band thing, on the other hand…" She faces me, bringing her leg up onto the cushion and tucking it under her ass. "I just really wish he'd give us a chance, you know? I'm starting to wonder if he has confidence in my talent at all. Maybe this whole concern for my mental stability is an excuse."

"I'm sure that's not what it is. He knows how talented you are," I assure her. "He's probably just worried about you entering that life. He does know firsthand how intense it is to be a rock star."

"I'm not trying to be a rock star to get famous." She flops her head back and stares at the ceiling. "I just want to perform onstage and share my art with people who want to listen."

"You're too beautiful for your own good."

"So are you."

We stare at each other until the heat of the moment becomes too much.

Looking away, I collect my guitar from the floor. "Lyric, we *will* get to perform. Even if it's not at your father's club opening; we'll get our chance one day."

"I know we will. I just wish it were sooner. You know how impatient I can be."

"Yes, I do," I agree, positioning the guitar on my lap.

She narrows her eyes at me, but then laughs. "I'm just anxious. That's all. No biggie."

"Anxious about what?"

Her attention drifts to the wall covered in albums. "I don't know. Stuff."

"Lyric Scott." I splay my fingers across her cheek and force her to look at me. "What's going on?"

"Did you just last name me?" She elevates her brows accusingly.

"Call it payback for all those times you've called me Shy Boy and dude. Now, fess up. What's going on? I can tell something's bothering you."

"I'm just worried that I might not have it in me, and then all of this," she gestures around the garage covered with albums, instruments, amps, and ashtrays, "will just have been a waste of my time."

"You do have it in you. Your voice, it's…" I don't even know how to describe the sound of Lyric singing. The sultry tone of her voice is almost unreal. "It's unearthly. Unreal. Beautiful."

A grin curves at her lips. "Unearthly? Wow, that's poetic. If I didn't know any better, I'd guess you were trying to flirt with me again."

I give a half shrug. "I'm just being truthful."

Her green eyes bore into me, and desire pulsates through my veins, desire I'm terrified to act on.

Just grab her and kiss her.

Crush your lips to hers.

Drink her soul

And give her yours.

"I know you are," she says. "And it's not a lack of confidence in my ability that I'm worried about. It's my confidence in my ability to perform in front of people other than you, Sage, and Nolan."

"You'll be fine, and I'll be there to help you."

"I know you will." Her grin broadens as she shifts her body toward mine, nearly bursting with excitement. "You should just start singing duets with me. Then I wouldn't have to worry about being up on stage, singing solo."

"You should probably hear me sing before you start making plans," I tell her, but she just stares at me expectantly. "I'm not going to sing for you." I lean over the armrest to prop my guitar against the wall. "I'm not a singer."

"Have you ever tried?" She inches closer, and strands of her hair tickle my cheek.

The feel of her warm breath and nearness sends a shiver through my body. Images of laying her down on the sofa and kissing her passionately flood my mind and make it almost impossible to breathe steadily, let alone reply to her question.

Swallowing hard, I shake my head.

"But you write lyrics."

My lips part in surprise. "How do you know?"

She chews on her lip, looking guilty. "Don't be mad at me, but there was this one time when you left your notebook open on your bed. I honestly thought it was just schoolwork and was going to shove it out of the way. Then I saw what was written on the opened page."

"Did you read the entire book?"

She places her hands on the armrest behind me, pinning me between her arms as if she's afraid I'm going to run. "I would never do that. I just read the one page then set it aside. It was good, though, what I read. Sad, but really, really moving. You have a hidden talent, Shy Boy. One I'll admit I'm a little jealous of." She wets her lips with her tongue.

I'm uncertain exactly what she's attempting to do—if she's unintentionally trying to turn me on or not. Regardless, my cock is getting hard inside my jeans. My body only gets more muddled when she moves near enough that her chest brushes mine.

"Which one was it?" I struggle to concentrate on the conversation as her body heat clouds my thoughts.

"Huh..." She's as equally distracted as I am.

"Which song was it that you read?"

"I think it was called 'You Devour Me.'" She stretches her arms farther toward the armrest, arching her back and aligning her chest, hips, and legs with mine.

I can't fucking breathe.

Focus.

Focus on something else.

Focus on the song.

"You Devour Me" is a song I wrote about her not too long after we shared our first kiss, when I was confused about what was going on inside me and thought I was going to lose my mind. So damn confused all the time, all I could do was write to free myself from the confusion. I ended up writing a lot. And wrote about Lyric frequently.

You seep into my skin, devour me whole.
Beg me to cave in, give in to what I fear.
You make my body burn. Make my heart bleed.
Make me feel alive. Make it so fucking hard to breathe.

Nothing feels right whenever you're near.
Everything feels wrong whenever you disappear.
Fuck, I can't figure out what you're doing to me.
What you make me feel. Was never supposed to be.

"We should sing it," she breathes against my mouth. "I could play guitar for one set, and you could sing." She sucks her lip between her teeth as her gaze zeroes in on my lips.

"I'm pretty sure I'm tone deaf." I fight an internal tug-of-war with my mind and body.

Take and devour her.

Deal with the consequences later.

Or push her away.

And drift farther away from having her.

"Then I could sing it," she says in a raspy voice I've never heard come out of her mouth before. It's like we're talking dirty without actually talking about anything dirty. "Unless that's weird."

"Weird?" *I have no idea what we're talking about anymore.*

"Yeah. I mean, it seemed like you wrote the song about someone. Maybe it's personal."

"I'm not sure I'm ready to sing it aloud. Maybe one day I'd be okay with you singing it, though." Maybe one day I'll be okay enough to admit the lyrics are about my true feelings for her. Maybe one day I'll actually be able to fully admit them to myself.

She hooks her arms around me. "I'm so glad you said that. It's such a good song." She squeezes me, crushing the air from my lungs.

Raveling You

My arms enclose around her waist and I nuzzle my face into the curve of her neck. She sighs contentedly as my fingers travel down her spine and sketch a delicate path along the bottom of her back. I bite my lip to restrain a moan when she shudders. "The Window" by Mars Volta fills up the silence between us as she nips at my earlobe with her teeth, and my body quivers uncontrollably.

"I know we never actually fully reached a conclusion to what was okay between us," she whispers with another graze of her teeth, "and what was not, but—"

I cut her off, turn my head, and press my lips to hers so roughly our teeth clank together. Probably the least sexiest kiss ever. Add that to the fact that I can't figure out what to do with my hands—never seem to be able to—and she should leave me high and dry. Instead she presses closer, rolling her hips against mine as she nips at my lip and tugs at my hair.

"You feel so good," she moans breathlessly as she rocks her hips again. "Is this okay? You're not feeling anxious, are you?"

Not this time. This time, I am way less stressed out. I feel way more in control over my head, at least for the moment, anyway.

Another mind-blowing movement of her hips and I damn near explode. Something possesses me—an urge I don't understand—and I'm suddenly flipping us over.

A quiet whimper escapes Lyric's lips as her back hits the sofa cushions.

"Are you okay?" I wiggle my body over hers, still feeling out of my element.

Push or pull?

Want or desire?

Stay or flee?

Her blonde hair looks like a halo around her head, her green eyes are glazed over, and her lips are swollen from the intense kiss. She's the most beautiful sight I've ever laid eyes on. Will ever lay eyes on.

"More than okay." She cups the back of my head and guides my mouth to hers for another passionate kiss.

Our tongues twine together as I grind my body against hers. A shudder then another grind. I feel like I'm dying inside, yet at the same time, fully alive. My body and mind are a walking contradiction, never wanting the same thing.

For the moment, my body ends up winning as I glide an unsteady hand up Lyric's dress. Her legs part, and I settle between her with my hand on her ass. She shivers, and her head falls back as she gasps.

Terrified, I start to pull away, but she reaches between us and places her fingers over mine, holding my hand there. I kiss her fiercely until my lips feel swollen then move my mouth down her neckline. Little whimpers and moans keep escaping from her lips the lower I delve. By the time I reach the top of her dress, I'm pulsating with need.

She rolls her hips against mine again as she grabs my hair. Glancing up, I slide one of the straps of the dress down while watching her expression. When her chin dips down, her hungry gaze collides with mine. She wants this, wants me. I don't even know how to process that fact, so I try not to, try not to think about anything as I slip the strap down and expose her breast.

"Oh, my God," I whisper. I'm as hard as a rock. Through the yearning, the fear is there, residing under my skin.

I won't give in. I won't give in.

Lyric grasps my hand that's still on her ass, but I manage to pull away. I take her other hand, and with our fingers linked, I move her arms above her head, then I lower my mouth to her breast, and suck her nipple into my mouth.

Her back bows, our bodies meld together. I'm about to lose it, yet somehow, I continue going, sucking and tracing circles with my tongue. Lyric gasps and moans and writhes underneath me until she finally cries out, stabbing her nails into my hands as she comes apart.

The pierce of her nails almost causes me to tumble into a memory.

See the darkness eating around you.

It will one day consume you.

Because we're not going to let you out of here

Until you're so ruined you'll never be good again.

No, no, no.

I don't want to see it.

I force the images out of my mind, returning to reality just in time to see Lyric blinking up at me.

"Are you okay?" she asks as she traces her finger across my collarbone.

I nod, still in shock over what just happened between us. "Are you?"

"I'm more than okay." Her hand glides down my spine to the bottom of my back, just above the waistband of my jeans, and her fingers play with the fabric of my boxers.

Every single one of my muscles wind into knots, and the moment begins to crumble.

I don't—can't—be touched.

She must see the terror on my face because she quickly removes her hand. "I'm sorry. When I go too far, just say so, okay—"

The sound of the door swinging open cuts her off. I swiftly jerk the strap of her dress over her shoulder, and then we both bolt upright, tugging our clothes into place. We don't move fast enough, and Nolan and Sage get a clear idea of what's been going on.

"Oh," Nolan says, glancing between Lyric and me. Then he busts up laughing, hunching over and cradling his stomach. "Dude, next time, lock the door."

Sage doesn't appear as amused. In fact, he seems really irate. I think about all the times I've caught him flirting with Lyric and checking her out and worry this might end up being one of those issues that breaks up the band.

"Do you want us to leave so you two can finish up?" Sage says flatly as he kicks the door shut.

Lyric combs her hair into place, calm as can be. "We're good, but thanks."

Sage's eyes land on me, burning holes into my head. "What about you? You good? Or do you still need to go into the bathroom and finish off?"

"Knock it off." I hate drama, and Sage is trying to stir it up.

A pucker forms at Sage's brow, but the confusion quickly disappears as he turns around. "I'm going to go outside and smoke." He storms out of the garage, slamming the door behind him.

An awkward silence forms between the three of us.

"I should go talk to him." I get up and head for the door while Nolan sits down on one of the stools and starts tuning his guitar.

"Are you sure you want to?" Lyric calls out after me. "It might be better to just let him have his hissy fit and get over it."

If Sage likes Lyric, then I'm not sure he's going to get over her. Lyric isn't the kind of girl you just get over.

"I'm just going to make sure he's okay." I slip out the door before she can say anything else.

When I find Sage, he's sitting on the hood of his truck, puffing on a joint.

"Are you sure you should be doing that?" I hoist myself on the hood and prop my feet on the bumper. "What if someone sees you?"

He takes a drag, traps the smoke in his chest, and then exhales. "I really don't give a shit who sees me." He holds the joint between his fingers, staring at his neighbor's house in the distance. "So, you guys are like a thing now?"

"I don't know." I tensely massage the back of my neck, unsure of what else to say to him.

He glances at me and arches a brow. "You don't know?"

I shrug. "We haven't really talked about it. Why are you so pissed about the idea, though?"

"Because I like her," he says simply as the stench of weed circles around us. "That's what I was actually trying to talk to you about. To see if you'd be cool with me dating her."

"Oh." I have no clue what to say to him.

We're quiet for a while as he tokes up. He offers me a drag, but like always, I never take it.

"Well," he finally says when we hear Nolan and Lyric blast the amp, "we should probably get inside."

We hop off the hood, and I follow him toward the garage.

"Are we cool?" I ask as he grips the doorknob.

"Sure." He shrugs as he takes another hit from the joint. "It's probably my own damn fault for waiting too long, especially when I could be where you two were headed."

How could he possibly know where Lyric and I are headed when I don't even know myself?

He opens the door. "Besides, I probably shouldn't get all tied up. Leaves room for groupies, right? That is, if we ever get a gig."

I laugh, even though I think he's only half joking.

When we enter the garage, Nolan and Lyric are rocking out on the guitars. Lyric is using mine, sitting on the edge of the sofa, while Nolan is the middle of the room, head banging.

As her fingers pluck the strings, Lyric's gaze finds mine. *Everything okay?* she mouths, playing chord after chord.

I shrug and mouth, *I think so.*

I cross the room and sit down beside her. They finish the song, and when the room goes quiet, Sage clears his throat.

"I'm sorry for being a dick," he apologizes to Lyric as he picks up his drumsticks.

"It's okay," she says with a small smile. "Just as long as you don't do it again. And you let us use my name for the band."

Sage plops onto the stool behind the drums and twirls his drumsticks. "What's the name?"

"Alyric Bliss?

"How'd you come up with that?" Nolan asks, unscrewing the cap from a bottle of water.

Lyric shrugs. "I just played with some words."

"It has your name in it," Sage points out with a bang of the symbol.

"So?" Lyric shrugs again. "My name is awesome."

Sage considers the name, bobbing his head up and down. "I kind of like the sound of it." He looks to Nolan who shrugs.

"I'm good with it." He takes a swig of water then sets the bottle down on the floor.

Sage glances at me. "What do you think?"

"I'm good with it." I grab my guitar from Lyric.

"I'm also going to work on creating a band logo," Lyric adds, cracking her knuckles. "Put my art talent to use."

"You're an artist?" Sage questions. "Since when?"

"Since forever," Lyric replies. "My mom's one, too."

"A woman of many talents," Sage muses thoughtfully as he taps a drumstick against the symbol.

"FYI, I put the *A* at the front of Alyric Bliss to stand for your name," Lyric whispers to me when Sage isn't paying attention. "Don't say anything, though. Sage won't use it if he knows. He'll make us change it to an *S*."

I can't help laughing.

Sage raises the drumsticks in the air and hollers, "Alyric Bliss." He moves to slam the drumsticks down, but freezes when the door swings open.

"Dad?" Lyric rises to her feet as Mr. Scott walks in. "What are you doing here?"

Sage's eyes widen and his lips part, completely star struck by the sight of the retired rocker. Nolan seems a little more at ease, but he still gapes.

Mr. Scott briefly glances at me, and I feel like he somehow knows what I was doing with his daughter, even though there's no way he possibly could. Our parents are clueless about our stolen kisses and heavy making out. If they did know, I'm sure they'd start making us keep our bedroom doors open when we're together and stop allowing Lyric to occasionally fall asleep in my bed.

Mr. Scott tears his attention off me and focuses on Lyric. "You said I needed to see you play. That, if I did, I would be begging for you to be in my lineup." He drops down in a fold-up chair near the door, reclines back, and folds his arms. "So, let's see your awesomeness."

Lyric looks at me helplessly. She's terrified of messing up, of her stage fright, of not impressing her father.

With my guitar still in hand, I step behind her and lean over her shoulder. "You've got this," I whisper, grazing my finger along the inside of her wrist. "It's just like the first time you sang in front of Sage. Pretend it's only you in the room."

She turns her head toward me, our lips almost touching. "Can I pretend you're in the room with me?"

I nod as my heart swells in my chest. Her words pierce my soul. How much she trusts me. How much I want her to trust me. How much I'm pretty sure we're not just friends anymore.

We're so much more.

Chapter 10

Lyric

I feel like I'm going to throw up as I raise the microphone to my mouth and prepare to sing in front of my dad. I'd rather run out the door and hide. What keeps my feet planted on the floor is what Ayden whispered in my ear.

Just him and me in the room.

No one else is here.

No one at all.

No one.

No one.

No one.

The music starts playing, a cover song we jam out to a lot. And with a deep breath, I open my mouth and sing.

Like the first time I sang in front of Ayden and Sage, my voice is slightly wobbly. I stabilize my tone quickly, though, and before I know it, I'm rocking out, putting on a show. I hit pitches I've never reached before and carry notes longer and more in control. Smooth is the first word that comes to mind when I'm finished. I performed smoothly.

"Well, what do you think?" I ask my dad after we finish the song.

I'm panting and sweaty like I always am after I sing. My heart dances lively in my chest as I wait in anticipation for his response. Usually, I can pick up what he's feeling, but right now, he appears neutral. I start to grow worried that maybe he didn't like it, that perhaps he's trying to figure out a way to let us down gently.

Stop being so self-doubtful!

I square my shoulders while I wait. When a grin spreads across his face, I release a trapped breath.

"You guys have a name yet?" he asks, leaning forward in the chair.

"Alyric Bliss," Sage responds, dropping his drumsticks to the floor.

"Well, Alyric Bliss," he stands to his feet, "you just got your first gig."

I run over and hug him, even though it's probably super unprofessional.

"Thank you, Daddy," I say, hugging him tightly.

"Don't thank me." He hugs me back. "As much as I

161

love you, I wouldn't have let you be in the lineup unless I thought you were good enough."

"Well, thanks for thinking we're good enough."

"More than good enough. You're really talented." He embraces me tighter and lowers his voice. "And I'm sorry for what happened the other day. You were right. Your mother and I should have told you."

"You're totally off the hook." I pull back to look at him. "Just as long as you never do it again."

He draws an *X* across his chest. "I promise."

I smile and step back. "Do you want to stick around and play with us for a while?"

"I was supposed to go home and help your mother with something." He rubs his jawline, tempted by my offer. "But I guess I could spare a few minutes."

A few minutes stretch into a few hours. By the time he leaves the garage, it's nearing eleven o'clock. He tells me to be home by one then adds that we might want to consider at least singing one of our own songs next week.

My stomach churns at the idea. Yeah, we've played a few of my songs, but the idea of spilling my soul out to a room full of people adds to my stage fright.

Fortunately, I don't stress about it for too long, because

162

Sage suggests that we go to Maggie's party. Suddenly, we're piling into Aunt Lila's car and heading toward the ritzy side of town near the docks.

"Who's DD?" Sage asks as we pull up to Maggie's dad's three-story mansion.

The party has moved outdoors; people are crammed on the front lawn and around the garage, and some have gathered near the numerous cars parked in the driveway. Music blasts from inside and flows through the air. Twinkle lights cover all the trees and dimly light up the yard.

"I'll be," Ayden and I say simultaneously.

"You two are no fun," Sage comments as he hops out of the car.

Nolan follows and the intoxicated people swallow up the two of them.

"So, tonight's been interesting." I remark when it's just Ayden and me in the car.

"Definitely." He stares at the party, and the lights from the trees reflect in his eyes.

"I mean, my dad randomly shows up and gives us our first gig. Sage gets mad for some silly reason when he catches us making out..." I trail off as Ayden raises his brows.

"You really don't know what that was about?" he questions skeptically.

"Should I?"

"Lyric," he starts.

I heave a sigh. "Fine, I know what it's about, but I don't want it to be about that. I don't want to have drama in the band." I pick at my sapphire nail polish. "Besides, I don't think of him as anything more than a friend, never have, especially when I like someone else." I smile at him, but my mood plummets when he frowns. "What's wrong?"

"Are you sure that you…?" He huffs out an aggravated breath. "Are you sure you want this—want me? We'd have to move really slow." He looks away, embarrassed. "I'm not even ready for you to touch me yet, at least not intimately."

"Of course I want you," I climb over the console and straddle his lap, "slow or fast or simple or complicated. I'll take whatever, just as long as you'll give it to me." I smile thoughtfully. "Hey, I'm totally putting that in a song when I get home."

He chuckles. "It would sound pretty good, wouldn't it?"

"It would," I agree. "You know, one day, we should write a song together and then sing it as a duet."

He chuckles again. "You are so ambitious sometimes."

"That is the best compliment you've ever given me." I lick my lips and move in to kiss him, hoping he doesn't lean away.

"What are we going to tell our parents about us?" he asks as my mouth inches toward his.

"I think we should hold off on telling them for a while; otherwise, they might put restrictions on our time together, and I don't want that."

"Agreed."

Our lips connect, breaths mingling.

I'm about to dive into the kiss when someone taps on the window. When I turn my head, I see William grinning at us from the other side.

"So, this is why you wouldn't hook up with me?" he asks with a shit-eating grin on his face. "Wow, I knew you were all about being nice to everyone, but seriously, you've lowered your standards to him?"

"You're just pissed off because he kicked your ass," I say haughtily. "Nice nose by the way."

"You little cunt." He reaches for the handle.

Ayden shoves me back into the passenger seat and gets out of the car as William opens the door. Ayden has him by a few inches, but William is definitely bulkier. Ayden once called William a steroid freak, and with his moodiness, I'm starting to wonder myself. Or perhaps he's just an asshole.

"You're going to walk away, back to the party, before I bash my knuckles into your face again." Ayden's voice is low and firm, and his hands are balled at his sides as he struggles to remain cool.

William's fingers dart to his crooked nose, probably remembering what happened the last time Ayden punched him. "Whatever. You two can go fuck yourselves," he spats, then storms back to the party.

Ayden slides back into the driver's seat and shuts the door, locking us in.

"Well, at least I got my first encounter with him over with." I blow out a shaky breath. I don't like the vile feeling stirring inside me.

"Tonight's been full of drama, hasn't it?" He tucks a strand of my hair behind my ear, and his fingers linger on my cheeks. "I won't let him hurt you."

"I can take care of myself, Ayden, but thank you. For

protecting me."

A smile touches his lips then he leans over the console to kiss me. But before our lips can reunite, his phone vibrates.

Sighing, he moves back to retrieve his phone and check the message. A frown etches on his face as he glances at the screen. "We have to go home."

"Why… We still have an hour and a half left before curfew."

"Because… the police are after a man that fits the description of the guy we saw that night standing in front of the house."

"Why are they after him? Was he hanging around outside your house again?"

His eyes are wide, sheer terror radiating from his pupils. "No he broke into my house."

Chapter 11

Lyric

We text Sage and Nolan, telling them they have to find their own ride home, then we leave the party. By the time Ayden and I arrive at the house, my parents and the entire Gregory family have gathered in the living room of my home because Fiona, Kale, and Everson are too scared to go home. So scared, in fact, that they all brought their sleeping bags and pillows over to spend the night.

After we walk in, they sit us down and tell us what happened.

When the Gregorys came home from dinner, Uncle Ethan caught the guy snooping around in Ayden's room. Before they could do anything, the guy dove out the window. Uncle Ethan chased him for a mile but lost him in the park where a neighborhood Christmas party was taking place. The police are currently searching for the man and dusting for fingerprints even though Uncle Ethan is pretty sure the guy was wearing gloves. The worst part, though, was the tattoo Ethan saw on the back of the man's neck—

black ink and circles around solid lined symbols. While he didn't get a really good look at it, he's pretty sure it's the same tattoo that Ayden has branded on his side.

"We're going to find a way to get that tattoo off you." Uncle Ethan says to Ayden as he paces the living room, more riled up then I've ever seen him. "We'll get you laser surgery or you can go get it covered up, but it's coming off."

"Fine by me," Ayden mutters, shutting his eyes and sucking in a breath.

"The police also want you, Lyric, and Ethan to go in and look at pictures," Aunt Lila says. "See if maybe someone can identify him."

"Okay," all three of us mutter simultaneously.

The room grows quiet as reality seeps in. The guy had the same tattoo, which means he has to be part of the group that held Ayden hostage three years ago.

"We should turn a movie on," Aunt Lila suggests to my mother, breaking the silence. "It might take everyone's minds off this and help them fall asleep."

My mother agrees and the two of them start rifling through the DVD collection while my dad and Uncle Ethan wander into the kitchen to make a snack for everyone.

Ayden remains pretty quiet as Lila asks everyone what they want to watch. His silence is concerning me. He says stress sets off his panic attacks.

I scoot close to him on the sofa. "Want to go up to my room and talk?" I whisper in his ear.

Ayden nods once then gets to his feet, pulling me up with him.

"Where are you going?" Everson asks. At fourteen-years-old, the kid is sassy for his age, but I prefer his sassiness over Kale's gaping, especially after what Ayden told me.

Lila glances up from a stack of DVDs on the coffee table. "Ayden, you can't go anywhere, not for a while, anyway."

"Lyric and I are just going up to her room, if that's okay?" he asks politely. "We need to work on some songs."

"Songs?" Lila asks, her face contorted with puzzlement.

"Did your father hire you, then?" my mother asks as she searches the couch cushions for the remote.

"Yep, he sure did." Even though the night ended stressfully, I still glow with excitement and nerves, knowing that, in less than a week, I'll be doing my first performance.

"Good. I'm proud of you." She discovers the remote near the fireplace. "Just make sure you're careful, okay? The environment at those kinds of things is very adult."

"Mom, I turn eighteen in two months. I'm pretty much an adult already."

"You'll always be my little girl, Lyric Scott."

"Aw, are you getting soft on me, Mom?" I dramatically touch my hand to my heart. "Usually, you're the tough one and Dad gets all emotional."

"I am the tough one." She sternly points the remote at me. "But I love you just as much as him, which is why I'm going to come to the performance and keep an eye on you."

I dramatically stomp my foot. "Crap, there goes my plan of doing drugs and hooking up with guys all night."

"Lyric Scott." Her eyes enlarge as she shoots a warning look, pressing that we have an audience. "There are children in the room."

"Not really." Fiona's been doodling in her sketchpad the entire time we've been home but stops drawing to chime in. "I'm the youngest and I'm almost fourteen, which hardly makes me a kid anymore."

"You are a child." Lila sternly points a finger at her. "No matter how hard you try, Fiona Gregory, no matter how much makeup you put on, you are still my little girl."

"You know," I intervene, offering my two cents. "I've often wondered why my mom and you and even Uncle Ethan and Dad use our last names when you're angry. I mean, it's not like we don't know who you're talking to if you just say our first names."

"Lyric Scott," Aunt Lila scolds me, but then smiles. "Fine, you have a good point, but like how you and Ayden hold hands all the time, using your last names when we're angry is something we're going to do." She glances at my and Ayden's clasped fingers.

Kale tracks her gaze and frowns, like he's just realizing Ayden and I do such a thing. On top of feeling awkward, I feel bad for him. I've had a ton of crushes over the last few years, and it never feels all that great when you realize nothing will ever happen with the person you're momentarily obsessed with.

Ayden's grip on my hand strengthens. "We should go get that thing done," he says to me.

"Thing?" Her attention descends to our hands. "I

thought you guys were going to work on a song."

"We are," I say, hurrying toward the doorway before they can stop us.

"Keep the door open!" she calls out after us.

"Do you think she knows?" I hiss as I steer Ayden toward the kitchen to grab a snack before we head upstairs.

"About what?" Realization clicks and his jaw drops to the floor. "You mean about us... kissing?"

I nod as we enter the kitchen. The air smells of cinnamon and hot chocolate and makes my mouth water. "Yeah, it seemed like she might have known about us."

"Known what about you?" my dad asks, his voice scaring the bejesus out of me.

I slam to a stop near the island, quickly realizing he and Ethan might have overheard us.

"Um, that Ayden and I haven't gotten any of our homework done over holiday break," I lie poorly.

My dad pops a chunk of chocolate into his mouth then trades a look with Ethan. "You two seem awful nervous right now."

I rack my brain for what to say and catch a whiff of cigarette smoke. *Jackpot!* My out.

"About as nervous as you two," I retort, scooping up a couple of pieces of fudge from off a platter on the counter-top.

"What do you mean?" The microwave beeps. "We're not nervous."

"Maybe you should be." I hand Ayden a piece of the fudge and stuff one into my mouth. "I can smell you from all the way over here." The chocolate melts in my mouth. So delicious. Aunt Lila makes the best fudge.

He removes a bowl from the microwave, then tenses. "I have no idea what you're talking about." He exchanges another look with Uncle Ethan.

"I can smell it on you, too," I tell Uncle Ethan and his expression plunges, his back stiffly straightening like a bolt of lightning just zapped him. "I'm not going to nark or any-thing. Just thought I'd let you know." I shovel a handful of candy from a glass dish then tug Ayden out of the room with me before anything else can be said.

"You've always known how to talk your way out of things," Ayden says as we ascend the stairway. "But I've never seen you make them squirm like that."

"If I didn't try something, then they would have pried the truth out of us with their parental mind control skills," I joke, pushing open my bedroom door.

I flip on the lights, wrestle out of my jacket, and scarf down the remaining candy. Then I kick my boots off and flop down on the bed.

"You want to talk about why you're so quiet?" I ask with my mouth full of candy gooeyness.

He shuts the door and slumps against it. "I'm just trying to process everything." He lets out a shaky breath. "Why the hell was the guy in the house? A guy who clearly has to be part of that group." He touches his side where his tattoo is hidden beneath his shirt.

I stretch out on my stomach, pondering the possibilities. "Maybe he wasn't part of the group," I say, trying to remain optimistic. "Maybe he just had a tattoo that looked the same. Maybe he was just breaking in to steal stuff and Uncle Ethan scared him off before he could take anything."

Ayden frowns. "There seems to a lot of maybes."

"I know." I sigh and bend my knees so my feet are in the air. "But I still don't get it. Say he's one of those people."

"Soulless mileas," he mumbles as he sinks to the floor, brings his knees up, and slumps his head against the door.

"That's what they're called."

Hearing the name of them makes the situation even more unsettling. "Okay, let's say he is part of this group and he was the guy outside staring at your window. He's obviously been watching you and the house, but then why break in when no one's home? To just go in your room? There had to be a point."

"Maybe he thought I was in there and was coming after me?"

"Maybe, but Aunt Lila and Uncle Ethan usually turn off all the lights when no one's home." I trace my finger across my lips. "What if he was looking for something else besides you?"

"Like what? I don't have anything. Nothing important anyway."

"What if he left something then?"

He lifts his head and cocks a brow. "Have you been reading mystery books again?"

"Yeah, so what?" I push up from the bed and kneel down in front of him. "It wouldn't hurt to look around your room, would it?"

He traces the scars on the back of his hand. "It might."

"I'll go look then." I start to get up.

176

He snatches hold of my arm and pulls me back down, swiftly shaking his head. "I'm not going to risk your safety over mine."

"They don't want me," I remind him. "I'll be okay."

"They want everyone." He continues to trace the pale scars, while dazing off over my shoulder. "They came from fingernails."

"What did?"

"The scars on the back of my hand. That and metal cuffs." When our gazes weld together, his grey eyes fiercely scorch. "Still want to go over there?"

My lips quiver as I nod, telling myself that it's just next-door and our parents will be only a yard length away. Everything will be fine. But Ayden seems like he believes the exact opposite, as if at any moment someone is going to charge through the door and steal us both.

"In the morning, we'll check things out," he says with uncertainty. "I'm not taking you over there when it's dark. And only hours after the guy was in the house. Besides, maybe the police will catch him by tomorrow."

"So, what do we do for the rest of the night then? Because we have to do something. Otherwise, we'll just sit around and drive ourselves crazy with worry." I sound innocent, but my body and mind are hyper aware that we're in my room with my bed only a few feet away.

He straightens his legs and rises to his feet. "We really could work on a song."

I perk up. "You want to write one with me?"

"We could try." He cracks the door, leaving it open like Aunt Lila said. "I'm not sure how good it'll be, though."

"I think we might rock it." I cross the room to my bookshelf. The bottom row is lined with a collection of CDs my dad gave me. "What's your choice of poison?" I ask as I skim the titles.

He crouches down beside me. "Something relaxing. I don't think I can handle any more stress tonight."

"Hmmm…" I thrum my finger against my lips then select a CD. Going over to my nightstand, I open the case, remove the disc, and feed the player my disc.

"What is this?" Ayden walks up behind me, causing my skin to tingle.

The sensation is insignificant to what I felt earlier today on Sage's couch. My very first orgasm, and it was better than any scenario I'd ever conjured up in my very creative mind.

I skip through the songs and land on one of my favorites. "'Civilian' by Wye Oak."

"Do I get a mark against me because I don't know them?" He tangles his fingers through my hair and sweeps the strands aside. Then he does something unexpected but amazing. He rests his chin on my shoulder. A gesture so small and plain an outsider wouldn't think twice about it.

Me, I think a lot about it.

So much my mind sparks like a hot-wired car.

"This is nice." I rest against his chest and his arms enclose around my waist. His nerves are still evident with the fumbling movement of his hands and his heart pounding against his chest and my back.

He places delicate kisses on my shoulder, savoring the taste of my flesh. My head uncontrollably falls back, my neck arched and exposed, seeking more of his gentle touches.

"Lyric," he whispers, his mouth moving against the arch of my neck. "I need you to promise me one thing."

I bob my head up and down, my eyes rolling into the back of my head as my eyelashes flutter. I would promise him anything right now.

"Promise me that if this gets to be too much—if at any point you feel like I'm bringing you down—you'll walk away."

"That will never happen."

"Just promise me, okay. I need to know that I'll never ruin the amazing person that you are."

Shaking my head, I spin around and loop my arms around the back of his neck. "You'll never ruin me. You add to my amazingness, not hinder it." His lips part in protest, but I talk over him, "But if you really need me to promise then I will. Just know that I'll never feel that way."

He seems somewhat satisfied by my answer.

"Now, no more stress." I grab his hand, push him back, then raise our arms and spin around like a ballerina. "Let's write beautiful lyrics together."

He laughs and twirls me around again. My dress spins around my waist, dancing with me, and my hair flows behind me like a flag in the wind.

After a few more twists, we hop on my bed and get situated with some pillows, a notebook, and a pen.

"I'll write the lyrics with you, but it's up to you to sing them." He fluffs a pillow then lies down beside me.

I prop up on my elbow. "For right now, I will. But one day in the future, I will get to hear you sing, Shy Boy."

"And what if I suck?"

"Then you suck, but at least I'll have gotten the chance to hear you."

"All right, just know that you've been warned."

I salute him. "You've done your duty, my dear friend. Now, what should we write about?"

He shrugs, rotating on his side and propping up on his elbow. "I don't know. What do you want to write about?"

We ponder our options while the song plays through and changes to the next.

"I never knew it could be like this," Ayden finally says, his lips quirking.

I'm not sure if he's talking to me or mumbling a lyric, but I write it down anyway.

His eyes drift to the ceiling as he ponders the next line. "Kissing the air from her lungs."

"*Her*, huh?" I pen what he said down. "Guess I'm a lesbian in this one."

He chuckles and I grin.

"And the heavens rain stars down on us." I scribble

across the paper.

"Pieces of shimmering gold around us."

"Pouring warmth all over us."

"Kiss me until I can no longer breathe."

"Raveling me up with you until I can hardly think."

That's how far we make it before we start making out on my bed. We stick to kissing and getting tangled in the sheets, but we break our lip lock the moment Ayden starts having trouble breathing.

I can tell he's upset that he has to force us to stop. I talk around the subject and eventually manage to sidetrack his thoughts.

A little past two o'clock, Aunt Lila pokes her head into the room and tells us we should go to sleep. She doesn't make Ayden leave, but she does open the door all the way.

We start to drift off a while later, lying face to face while Ayden strokes my cheek and stares deeply into my eyes.

That's the last thing I remember before the screaming starts.

Chapter 12

Lyric

Screaming.

Screaming.

Screaming.

At first, I think I'm dreaming.

But when my eyes shoot open, I realize I'm not.

I search frantically for where the noise is coming from. But the lights are off and nightfall is heavy and thick against my vision. The yelling is coming from somewhere close. Somewhere in my room. But I have no idea where.

I sit up in my bed and fumble around in the dark until I feel my lamp. I tug on the cord, clicking it on. Light flows around my room and I realize Ayden isn't in my bed. The screaming has stopped, though.

I hold my breath, waiting anxiously for someone to run into my room, because someone had to have heard it. But my house is fairly big and the walls are fairly soundproof and sometimes sounds get muffled.

183

When no one shows up, I stumble out of bed and peek under my bed, then head for my closet, the only other place he could be in my room. When I open the door, Ayden is huddled in the corner with his arms wrapped around his knees. He's rocking back and forth, staring at the wall. His eyes are huge, glossy, dazed, and out of touch with reality.

I cautiously approach him, worried I might spook him if I move too quickly. The closer I get, the more I realize he's not awake; he's sleep walking. Everson used to do it when he first arrived at the Gregory's. He actually walked over to our house one night and tried to get inside. My mother thought it was an intruder and almost called the police. Thankfully, Aunt Lila found him before that happened. She gently guided him home, telling my mother that, if it ever happened again, to not wake him up; he'd get hysterical if she did.

Deciding I need to find Aunt Lila, I turn around.

"Where are you going?" Ayden mumbles. "You can't leave here."

I freeze and peer over my shoulder. He still seems in the same condition, spaced off in dreamland.

"I'm just going to get your mom," I say quietly, turning to leave again.

"Your mom's dead," he utters. "She's dead, and she left you here to rot with us."

An eerie chill slithers up my spine, like a bolt of electricity zapped me in the back.

"Ayden, my mom's fine. She's just asleep like everyone else."

"There's no sleeping in this house." His eyes are fastened on the spot of carpet in front of his feet. "We don't sleep, not until the ritual."

A massive lump wedges in my throat. Absolutely terrified and with no clue what to do, I leave him there and race down the hallway to my parents' room, hoping he doesn't go anywhere. I give my mother a shake to wake her up then tell her what's happening. She immediately stumbles out of bed and runs into the guest room to wake up Aunt Lila.

"Where is he?" Aunt Lila asks, hopping out of bed and throwing on her robe.

I point down the hallway. "In the closet in my room."

She races into my room with my mother and me following. She sticks her head inside the closet, and her shoulders relax.

I relax, too, but only a little because I can still remem-

185

ber what Ayden said to me. His words are an echo in my head. His mother was dead while he was with those people. He wasn't allowed to sleep until the ritual.

What the hell?

"Come on, sweetie," Aunt Lila speaks tenderly as she holds onto Ayden's arm and guides him out of the closet. Ayden is still asleep and can hardly stay on his feet as they make a winding path to my bed.

Once he's lying down on the mattress, Lila turns to me. "Lyric, would you mind if I slept on the floor?" she asks in a hushed tone. "I want to keep an eye on him, but I'm worried that, if I try to get him into the guest room, I might wake him up."

"Lyric can sleep on the sofa." My mom pets my head like she used to do when I was child.

"Yeah, of course." I grab a folded up quilt from the trunk at the foot of the bed.

"Thank you." Aunt Lila draws the comforter over Ayden.

"I'll go get a sleeping bag for you," my mother tells Aunt Lila then hurries out of the room.

I start to follow her but Aunt Lila calls me back.

"What exactly happened?" She momentarily stares out

the window then tugs the cord and closes the blinds.

I shrug, hugging the quilt to my chest. "I was woken up by a scream and found him in the closet."

"Did he ... say anything to you?" Her question is casual as well as her demeanor, but it almost looks forced.

"He was muttering some stuff." I omit the details, figuring I'll tell Ayden in the morning and let him decide if he wants to tell her.

"Are you sure you couldn't understand what he was saying?" She studies me from across the room.

I shake my head. Something feels off. It's like she already knows the answer to her question and only wants me to confirm it. "I'm going to get set up on the sofa."

I leave the room, feeling strange and really uncomfortable in my own home. The feelings amplify when I realize I'll be sharing the living room with Kale, Everson, and Fiona.

The three of them are sprawled out on the floor, fast asleep in their sleeping bags. It's like a maze to get through them to the sofa.

"Is he going to be okay?" Fiona suddenly asks while I'm making a bed on the couch near the fireplace.

I jump from the sound of her voice. "I thought you were asleep."

"I was, but then Ayden woke me up." She rolls over in her sleeping bag and stares at me. A fire is crackling, my parents' heat source during the mild winters in California. Fiona's eyes glow orange, the flames reflecting in her pupils. Dark strands of hair poke out of her braided hair at every angle.

"You heard his screaming?" I ask.

She shakes her head. "No, I felt it."

My brows knit. "I'm not sure what you're talking about."

"Most people don't." She turns over like nothing about the conversation is strange.

Although, it is.

The entire night has been strange.

I just cross my fingers, hoping that, by morning, things will have returned to normal.

Chapter 13

Ayden

"I don't know what to say," I mumble to Lyric the next day after the break-in.

It's late in the evening and the pale pink glow of the sunset streams though my window. We're in my bedroom, searching for something the guy might have left, but so far, we have come up empty-handed. For the last five minutes, Lyric has been explaining to me what happened last night, how I talked to her in my sleep. The things I said to her ... I feel so embarrassed. She has to be afraid of me now, right?

While I don't give a reason aloud as to what caused my sleepwalking and talking, I have a theory that perhaps it has something to do with the amnesia session. My therapist told me that it could cause an increase in night terrors and problems with sleeping

"You don't need to say anything," Lyric says as she hauls my dresser away from the wall and peers behind it. "I just wanted to let you know what happened so you can decide if you want to tell your mom and dad."

"You said Lila was acting strange?" I flatten myself on the floor on my stomach to check under my bed. Having no idea what I'm searching for, the task seems pretty much pointless, though.

"She was acting like she knew you told me stuff about your past." Lyric purses her lips as she glances around my room. "If I was a creepy guy trying to leave something in a room, where would I put it?"

I push to my feet. "I don't know. I'm still not convinced that's why he was in here, anyway."

"Maybe." She flops down on my unmade bed, seemingly unsure about something. "Has Fiona ever said anything weird to you before?"

"Like what?" I rummage around in my nightstand drawer, but the only thing in there is my notebook full of lyrics.

"I don't know." She shrugs. "She just said something strange to me last night, something about feeling you scream instead of hearing it."

"That's strange, but she kind of marches to the beat of her own drum." I shut the drawer. "Ever since I moved in, I've noticed she draws butterflies obsessively. She says she can't get them out of her head."

"What's her story?" Lyric asks, looking under my bed-spread. "I know she came here when she was seven, but that's about it."

"Her mother was a drug addict like mine. She got taken away and ended up here. That's about all I know."

"Strange." Lyric contemplates something as her gaze deliberately sweeps my room. "Wait a minute... Are you sure he didn't *take* anything? Like maybe something Aunt Lila and Uncle Ethan didn't know you had?"

"I have a couple of things..." I open the top drawer and my heart skips a beat. "My knife is gone."

"The one you were trying to give Rebel Tonic?"

"Yeah, but why would he take that," I glide the drawer shut and rub my jawline, "out of all the things in this house that have value?"

"Maybe it wasn't for value purposes." Her skin suddenly pales as her eyes widen.

"What's wrong?" I ask, sitting down on the bed beside her.

"Don't be mad, okay, but last night, after the incident, I couldn't sleep, so I did some searching on the Internet about the soulless mileas." She collects my laptop from the nightstand, sets it on her lap, and boots up the screen. "I think I remember something about rituals and needing an object that belongs to the person the ritual is for."

"Why?"

"Hold on." Her fingers hammer against the keys as she types something in the browser then pulls up a page. "Read here." She taps her finger against the screen

Leaning over her shoulder, I skim the paragraph then frown. "Where did you find this website?"

"After like ten searches, it popped up." She shudders. "It says they need something off you too... like a belonging you carry or fingernails—weird stuff like that. It's so crazy. That people do this ... it gives me chills."

I rub my eyes and reread the paragraph again. "It's pretty vague about what the rituals are for."

"You talked about a ritual last night," she says cautiously. "Do you remember anything about it?"

A hot branding iron,

melting the flesh.

Forever marking you with our sins.

Little images sear inside my brain, ironically while I'm not in therapy. My fingers graze the homemade tattoo hidden beneath my shirt and distorted memories jolt through my mind. This mark was their mark. The mark of their group… What I would give to get rid of the ink on my skin, forget it was ever put on me, forget what it symbolizes— pure evil. "It might have something to do with this, but that's about all I can remember." I lower my head into my hands as my temples throb. Between this, the guy breaking in, and still no response from Rebel Tonic, I have a headache. "We need to tell Lila and Ethan about this."

Lyric slams the laptop shut. "Okay, but you also need a break." She stands up and slips a hand around my wrist, giving my arm a gentle tug. "How about we go get ready for the art show? We probably can head out there soon, too, if you're ready?"

"I'm not sure I'm allowed to go to that anymore. Lila said something about me staying home as much as possible."

"She's going to the art show, so I'm sure it'll be okay."

"How do you know that?"

"Because I was eavesdropping on her and my mom this morning and heard them talking about it?" She frees my wrist when I finally get up from the bed. "I guess Aunt

Lila is catering the event."

"Hear anything interesting?" I grab my blue hoodie from the closet.

"Not really." She frowns, disappointed. "They mostly just talked about the type of cake to serve and what wine my mom wants."

"I really should press her more about that letter." I slide my arms through the sleeves of my jacket.

"But you won't." She opens my bedroom door. "Because you're too nice."

"I just don't want to come off sounding ungrateful." I follow her out of the room and down the hallway. "Especially with everything that's been going on. They have to be stressed out and I'm the one causing that stress."

"I'm sure they don't look at it like that." She slips her fingers through mine as we head downstairs to the kitchen. "I mean, my parents have put up with a lot of shit from me over the years, and I know for a fact they still love and want me. It comes with being a parent. Unconditional love no matter how much of a pain in the ass your kids are. And besides, this thing going on isn't your fault. It's completely out of your control."

"I still brought it into their lives."

"Yeah, but like I heard Aunt Lila say that night, they knew it was a possibility that this could happen and they still chose to adopt you." She gives my hand a comforting squeeze. "That's how special you are."

Even though I don't entirely agree with her, I brush my lips against hers. "Thank you."

"Thank you," she says, then she grabs the back of my head and fiercely kisses me back.

Her tongue slips out and parts my lips, causing a shudder to ripple through my body. A good shudder. One that makes me excruciatingly ache inside, long for more.

Suddenly, the door bangs shut. Lyric and I jump apart, breathless and gasping for air. Lila strolls into the kitchen with grocery bags in her hands.

"Oh good, I was just about to go look for you two," she says, dropping the bags on the countertop. "I need your help."

"With what?" Lyric asks, still holding my hand as she roams over to the counter.

Lila undoes the buttons on her coat and shucks it off. "With my event tonight. I had a few waitresses cancel and I need fill ins."

"You want us to mingle with my mother's pretentious clients." Lyric scrunches up her nose.

"They're not pretentious." Lila digs around in the bag and starts pulling out cans of condensed milk and stacking them on the counter. "They're artists, like you."

Lyric sits down on a barstool. "And I'm very pretentious."

Lila shakes her head, but smiles. "Oh Lyric, you remind me so much of your father sometimes. Always so full of sarcasm."

"Why thank you," Lyric replies, beaming with pride. "Because of your compliment, I'll give you a free night of my ever-so-awesome waitressing skills."

A laugh slips from my lips as I sit down beside her. "Guess that means you get mine, too," I tell Lila. "But mine aren't so awesome."

"That's okay." She throws the empty bag into the drawer. "At this point I'll take whatever I can get."

We start opening the cans of milk while Lila whisks eggs in a bowl, giving us directions on how to make cheese fondue. After a few minutes, Lyric whispers for me to tell Lila about the knife.

I loathe giving her more bad news, knowing she's only

going to get more stressed than she already is. I still recap the details, and Lila rushes out of the kitchen to call the detective and tell him.

"She seems upset." I open the fridge to grab a stick of butter.

"Of course she's upset." Lyric takes the butter from me and drops the stick into a small plastic bowl. "You're her son and some creepy dude snuck into your room and stole a knife from you because he believes in some icky ritual."

"We don't know that for sure," I tell her as she places the bowl into the microwave and presses the timer.

"I'm betting that's what the detective will say to her. They're investigating this group, right? They have to know about their rituals."

I hate that she's probably right about the group and the rituals. That she knows so much about this. That stuff like this exists in our lives.

When Lila returns to the kitchen a minute later, her eyes are bloodshot and her cheeks are streaked with the remnants of tears.

"Ayden, you need to make sure that you have someone with you at all times for the next few days." She goes right back to mixing.

Lyric and I trade a look from across the kitchen island.

"How come?" Lyric aligns the lid of the can with the opener and opens the top. "Because the man still hasn't been caught?"

"Yes. It's just a safety measure until they can track down the guy and find out if he's part of this group—get a positive ID on him. They dusted for fingerprints but nothing came up." Lila taps an egg against the side of the bowl and separates the shell. "The detective brought up the therapy sessions and wants to have another visit to discuss how they're going. He said we could do it when you guys go down to look through some photos."

"I don't know why he wants to visit about that. Nothing's changed. I still can't remember," I mumble as the microwave dings.

"Honey, that's not your fault." Lila retrieves the bowl of melted butter from the microwave. "You're doing everything you can by trying."

I nod, unable to speak. I feel like such a failure over the fact that I've gotten nowhere with my memories because my fear of remembering is hindering the progress.

"Ethan's going to have to go to the concert with you

guys," Lila adds as she pours the butter in with the eggs. "I mean, we were going to go already, but he's going to have to be backstage with you, to keep an eye on things."

"Are you sure this is just for safety measures?" Lyric questions as she pries the top of another can open, trading a suspicious glance with me.

"Of course. What else would it be for?" she asks, wiping her hands on a towel.

Excellent question. If they're not even positive who this man is or why he broke into the house? I think of my brother and how his body was found by that house.

Maybe that's what this is about.

Maybe Lila knows the real reason the man was in the house.

Maybe he was coming after me.

Chapter 14

Lyric

The next week passes rather quickly, but that might just be because I'm stressed out. We all are. Even at my mother's slamming art show, we were all a wreck. Fiona kept saying she had a feeling someone was watching us, or more specifically Ayden. After what she said that night, the girl has utterly creeped out.

Most days, everyone just kind of hangs out at the house, waiting for news that never gets delivered. Ayden and I are only allowed to be by ourselves when we're at band practice, a place that's quickly becoming our sanctuary through all of this, even though we work our butts off to learn one of the songs I wrote. Actually, the one Ayden and I wrote together.

After a lot of contemplating and Ayden refusing to let us sing one of his songs, I decide we should do the one we wrote. We had to complete it first, though, which took us an entire night, a six-pack of Dr. Pepper, and an endless amount of gummy worms.

But we did it.

Saturday night the tension in our lives briefly lifts like thinning fog. Because Saturday night is club opening night and our band's first gig. I'm ecstatic the entire day until we're actually at the club. Then reality kicks me in the face.

"Oh, my God, I think I'm going to puke," I whisper as I peek out onto the stage. "There are so many people out there."

"You'll be fine." Ayden rubs my back. "And just remember, only you and I are in the room."

Easier said than done when there are two hundred plus people buzzing with energy all crammed into one room. We're the first band up, too, something I sarcastically thanked my dad for.

"I'm suddenly wondering why I begged to do this so much." My eyes remain fixed on the floor. In the midst of the madness, near the bar, I spot my mom and Aunt Lila throwing back shots. Awesome. Guess Ayden and I are going to be DD since they were our ride here.

Uncle Ethan and my dad are around, shuffling people here and there, dictating what to do. The last time I saw my dad, he looked like a wreck, his bedhead/fauxhawk look in full form. I'd feel bad for him, but he's always said opening a club has been a dream of his for the last ten years, so I figure all the stress has to be worth it.

Most dreams are, right?

"Because it's your dream," Ayden reminds me as his hands travel up to my shoulders. His fingers work their magic, unwinding the knots in my muscles. "You can do this, Lyric. I know you can. You're the bravest person I know."

"Then you clearly don't know yourself."

"I'm not brave at all," he utters quietly. "I couldn't even make it through the start of my amnesia therapy without freaking out."

I embrace his touch as his arms circle my waist. "You'll get there. It'll just take some time."

"Tell that to Detective Rannali. He's getting super pushy about doing more sessions, like the entire case is riding on it. I don't get it, though. Even my therapist says the therapy isn't a guarantee, that there's a chance it won't work."

"Fuck Detective Rannali. It's easy for him to be pushy and expectant when he's not the one lying in that chair, facing what you are."

"But I don't even know what I'm facing." He rests his forehead against the back of my head, and his erratic breathing tickles the back of my neck. "I'm scared of what I'll see."

It's the first time he's flat-out admitted he is afraid. I wish I could take away his fear, wish I could free him from his pain.

"I'm here for you if you ever need to talk." It's all I can offer him, but I hope it's enough.

"I know." He grazes his lips across the back of my head. "Can we talk about something else now? Before I get all riled up."

I nod. "Um, did you see all the freaking musicians when we walked in? I seriously about died."

"Yeah, your dad's got mad connections."

"Sage is totally working it, too. He went right for the first girl he saw. I think she plays drums for one of the bands. I'll give it to him. She's pretty hot."

Ayden chuckles under his breath. "I love how you can openly say stuff like that, but just so you know, you look hot," he whispers in my ear, his breath hot on my skin.

I shiver from the caress of his breath and glance down

at my boots, netted tights, and plaid dress that hugs my body. My hair is down, black liner frames my eyes, and my lips shine with gloss.

"So do you." I whirl around to face him. His black hair hangs in his eyes, he's wearing the leather collar because I suggested it would be fun to wear for one night, and he has on a red shirt and black jeans held up by a studded belt. "My gothically adorable friend."

"You know, I think we should create a Lyric Scott dictionary and sell it online."

"We'll definitely have to look into that," I agree, fiddling with the collar on his neck. "I have so many more words sloshing around in my head."

I angle my head up towards his face. When our gazes fasten, our mouths magnetize toward each other. My breathing quickens and so does his. His dark eyes smolder with passion, and my skin hums with nearly unbearable heat. God, I want to kiss him all the time. It's crazy how much I want to kiss him.

This is how it's been between us for the last week. The moment we look at each other, we start making out and are unable to keep our hands off each other. I seriously feel like I have no control over myself anymore, and I'm kind of glad. I love, love, love losing myself in him.

I always have to be careful, though. Ayden has no problem with touching me, but I can't even slip my fingers up his shirt without sending him into a panic attack.

"You guys about ready to go on?" Uncle Ethan's voice instantly puts a lid on the moment.

We push apart, our breathing ragged. We turn to the side, and Ayden immediately withdraws his hands from my waist the moment he catches sight of Uncle Ethan's questioning expression.

"Um…" Ayden struggles with what to say.

"You're on in five." Uncle Ethan's attention flicks between the two of us before he hurries off toward the hallway where the rest of the bands are hanging out.

"Do you think he saw us?" Ayden asks worriedly as he faces me again.

I shrug. "I'm not sure. It kind of looked like it."

"What are we going to do if he did?"

"I don't know. He might not say anything to anyone. This is Uncle Ethan we're talking about. He rarely says anything."

"Yeah, but us about to kiss…" Ayden makes a wary

face. "I kind of doubt he'll keep quiet about that."

I open my mouth to tell him not to stress about it when Sage and Nolan come strolling up.

"This is so fucking awesome." Nolan bounces up and down on the balls of his feet, pumped up.

Sage leans around me to get a glimpse of the crowd. "Dude, the place is packed."

Place.

Crowds.

People watching me.

Watching me sing.

What if I suck?

I'm suddenly reminded that I have bigger problems than whether or not Ethan is going to out my and Ayden's relationship.

My stomach churns. "I think I'm going to throw up." I slap my hand across my mouth and push past Ayden, running into the restroom. I lock myself in the stall, drop to my knees, and puke up every ounce of the chicken I ate for dinner.

My belly is empty by the time I sit down on the floor.

"I can't do this," I mutter. "I really can't."

A moment or two ticks by, then I hear the click of

heels on the other side of the stall.

"Lyric, are you in here?" my mother hisses.

"Yeah," I say with a groan. "I think I'm too sick to go on stage, though."

She gives the stall door a shake. "Open up. Now."

I kneel up and unlatch the door then sit back down. She walks in with a glass half full of wine, and I notice her eyes are a little glazed. She takes one look at me then shuts the stall.

"You have to do this." She tears some tissue from off the roll and hands it to me.

"I know. I know. Or Dad will hate me." I dab the sides of my mouth and under my eyes then toss the tissue into the toilet.

"No, because you'll regret it if you don't." She pats the top of my head. "Trust me, your dad will forgive you if you bail. Will he be upset? Probably for a while, but he loves you too much to stay mad at you. But trust me when I say that regret is much harder to get over."

"You're speaking from personal experience, aren't you?" I stare up at her, the woman who shares the same eyes as me and is probably one of the coolest people I know. I look up to her for living her dream of becoming an artist.

She nods. "I am. There's a lot of stuff I have and haven't done in the past that I wish I could do differently."

I heave a weighted sigh. "Fine, I'll do it, but only because your pep talk is scaring me." I get to my feet, and then we exit the stall. I stop by the sink to wash my hands while my mom sets her wineglass down on the counter to fix her lipstick. While she's not paying attention, I pick it up and take a few swallows.

"Lyric Scott," she scolds, but I can tell she's working hard to be angry. "Don't ever do that again."

"Okay." I hand the glass back to her as the alcohol swims through my veins. I feel slightly mellower, but not a whole lot. I still manage to exit the bathroom and walk backstage where Sage, Nolan, and Ayden are waiting.

"You going to be okay?" Ayden asks, brushing my matted hair from my forehead.

I nod, but don't say anything as vomit burns at the back of my throat again. "No regrets. No regrets. No regrets," I chant under my breath.

"What are you saying?" Sage asks, semi-distracted by the stage.

"Nothing." I turn my back to him and keep chanting until we're called out.

"This is it," I whisper to myself. Then I raise my chin, square my shoulders, and march out onto the stage.

The lights are blinding, and the crowd is eagerly cheering, even though they have no clue who we are. I remember all the times I've cheered bands on and wonder if this is how any of those singers felt, as if they'd swallowed a thousand butterflies on crack.

Ayden and Nolan plug their guitars in and do a quick tuning and sound check. Sage does a few warm up beats while I stand in front of the microphone and adjust the height of the stand an unnecessary amount of times.

Then the strum of a guitar ripples through the amp and floats over the crowd. The entire room silences and people stare at me, waiting to be dazzled by my talent.

I'm supposed to say something. My dad told me what it was, but I can't remember.

"Um... we're Alyric Bliss," I murmur into the microphone, and my dad's words gradually come back to me. "And thanks for coming out. This one's called 'Raveling You'. "

Something as easy as a few sentence makes my knees threaten to buckle. I grasp the stand with my sweaty palms as Sage taps his drums. Then the three of them are playing, creating a flawless tune that swirls together and kisses the air. I just hope I don't fuck it up when I open my mouth.

The intro is pretty long, so I have to wait a seemingly endless amount of time before I sing, but the moment finally arrives.

I take a deep breath and part my lips.

"I never knew it could be like this, never thought such desire was possible, kissing the air from his lungs." My lips quirk at my slight word variation. "And the heavens rain stars down on us, pieces of shimmering gold around us, pouring warmth all over us. Kiss me until I can no longer breathe. Raveling me up with you until I can hardly think. God, please fucking kiss me before I crumble to pieces."

I move back as Ayden's guitar takes over. I suck in a few breaths, feeling less nervous. My voice is balanced, surprisingly smooth. Although, the next part will test it. The words move fast, and I have to push my voice to a near scream. In practice, I rocked it, but I'm worried now. My throat feels like sand paper after puking.

I step up to the mic again, grip the stand, and run my

fingers through my hair as some guy whistles at me from the crowd. "You make me weak. You make me strong. You make me ache. You make me feel so wrong. You make me burn for just a taste. You make me, make me, so fucking insane!" My voice carries flawlessly over the room.

And I can't help myself.

I smile, realizing this dream of mine just might be possible.

I create magic for the next forty-five minutes, and by the time we're finished, I feel like I'm glowing.

"Thank you!" I shout into the microphone then bounce off stage with the biggest smile plastered on my face.

My skin is damp, I reek of sweat, and I'm the happiest I've been in a long time. I hug Sage and Nolan after we make it backstage, and then I throw my arms around Ayden and hug the crap out of him.

"That was so much fun," I say, then throw my head back when he lifts me up off the ground and spins me around and around.

"You were amazing," he whispers in my ear, sneaking a bite of my earlobe.

"So were you." I kiss his cheek, and then he plants my

feet back down on the floor.

"Who wants to celebrate?" Sage's pumps a fist into the air, grasping a bottle of champagne.

"Where'd you get that?" I ask. "Did you steal it from one of the other bands or sneak it out from the bar?"

"Does it really matter?" He moves to pop the cork, but to no avail, showing his lack of experience with champagne bottles.

"Dammit, let me go find an opener." He strolls off, putting swagger in his step as he passes by a few older women batting their eyelashes and grinning at him.

"Oh, the life of a rock star." Grinning, I shake my head. "He's going to be a handful. Isn't he?"

"Probably," Ayden agrees with amusement. "Every band has one, though."

"So what do we do now?" My mind promptly conjures up very creative and vivid images.

"We could exchange our belated Christmas presents," he suggests. "It might be fun."

"I thought we were going to do that later? When we are happy."

"You look pretty happy right now."

"But what about you?"

"I'm happy just seeing you happy." When I hesitate, his brow cocks. "Do you really want to wait even longer? Or are you just procrastinating because you don't have mine?"

"I actually do." Which is the truth. But the present isn't bought so I'm uncertain how much Ayden will like it. Still, it did come from the heart. "Alright, let's do this. Hand it over."

"I don't have it with me." He nods his head at the bar. "But we can go get our moms and head home and I'll give it to you. Lila's looking pretty tipsy anyway."

I stick out my elbow and he links arms with me. "Sounds like a deal."

An hour later, Ayden and I are in my bedroom on my bed with the door open. Music is floating from my stereo and a soft trail of light flows from my lamp. My mom and Aunt Lila are downstairs with Kale, Everson, and Fiona, drunkenly chatting so loud we can hear them all the way upstairs.

"They're trashed," Ayden remarks as he tosses my present in the air like a baseball. It's small, about the size of mine, with shiny silver and purple wrapping paper.

"Not as bad as they were that one New Year's." My present for Ayden is secured in the palm of my hand. I'm nervous to give it to him. I don't know why. Maybe because the gift kind of means something? "Remember how giggly they were. The sounded like two silly teenage girls."

"You're a teenage girl," Ayden reminds me with a clever grin.

I smack my forehead with the heel of my hand. "Duh. Thanks for reminding me. I almost forgot."

He shakes his head, half grinning. Then he shoves his hand in my direction, presenting his gift. "You open yours first."

I snatch the present from him, tear open the paper, and lift the lid from the box. Inside are two leather bands with the words *Endlessly Yours* engraved on them.

"You mentioned once that your parents used to have leather bands that said forever on them and how they used to be best friends like us," he explains as I stare inside the box. "I remember how happy you looked when you told me about it and how you said that one day you were going to be with a guy that would get you something like that. I didn't want to make them exactly the same, though, so I went with endlessly yours."

I'm quiet for a lengthy amount of time, mainly because I'm way too emotionally overwhelmed to speak.

"You don't have to wear it if you don't want to," he says self-consciously. "Or you can keep them both and give the other to someone else one day."

I finally find my voice. "You said 'how they used to be best friends like us'."

"Huh?"

"Just barely. You said that we used to be best friends like how my parents used to be friends."

Pink colors his cheeks. "Well, I didn't really mean it like that. We're still best friends now, like your parents are, too. I just meant that we were like them in the sense that we used to be friends but now we're..." He scratches at the back of his neck, glancing at the door like he wants to bolt.

I place my hand on his arm. "We're more than friends, Ayden." When I withdraw my hand, he turns his head and looks at me. I take the bracelets out of the box, slide one on my wrist, then slip the other on his. "And I think this is going to prove it even more." I hand my present to him.

He gingerly rips off the paper then opens the tiny box.

"We think so alike it's frightening." He removes the two faded leather bracelets. Each one is engraved with *Forever*.

"Definitely, but I like that we do."

He puts the band on his wrist, then his fingers circle my arm and he slips the other bracelet on my wrist. His fingertips are right above my pulse and I wonder if he can feel how rapid my heart is racing. "Endlessly yours forever," he says, staring at the bracelets together.

"The ones I gave you actually belonged to my parents," I say when he doesn't release my wrist. "My mom gave them to me the other day when I asked her for present ideas. It kind of makes me wonder if she knows about us, since the bracelets are so symbolic to her and my dad's relationship."

"After tonight, I'm pretty sure Ethan might be wondering if something's up, too."

"I hope they don't know yet." My gaze flicks to the door then a smile curves at my lips as I lean in. "I like being able to be in my room alone with you." I stop when our lips are an inch away. "Thank you for my present."

"You're welcome… And thanks—" He eliminates the space between our mouths, cutting himself off.

I grab at his shirt and pull him down as I lie back on

my bed. Our tongues entwine as our bodies align. When our chests collide, my heart slams inside my chest and knocks against his unsteady heartbeat. His hands skate across my body, along my curves, the arch of my breast, and my hips, his fingers tremulous as he rocks against me.

I moan and my fingers form a mind of their own, wandering, wandering, wandering to the bottom of his shirt. I want to touch him. Savor the feel of his skin, bask in every part of him like he's doing with me. My fingers delve under the hem, caress his skin, fleetingly relishing his smooth, solid muscles. But then those muscles tauten along with the rest of his body.

I quickly pull my hands out. "Sorry," I breathe against his lips.

"It's okay." His voice is raspy, his chest forcefully rising and falling. "Can you just touch me on the outside of my shirt?"

"Of course."

"I'm sorry," he sputters, battling for oxygen.

I cup his face between my hands. "Don't be sorry… You're perfect… Everything's perfect." *And I think I might be in love with you.*

217

The thought strikes me like bolt of lightning. Out of nowhere. So startling that I don't dare utter it aloud. Too afraid. Of how he'll react. Of how I'll react.

Instead, I just keep kissing him and falling.

Deeper, deeper, deeper

Into another world.

Where I don't even know who I am anymore.

But it's not a bad thing.

Just terrifying and confusing.

My head is so foggy yet clear.

My heart so alive, so vibrantly beating.

My body so needy, desperately seeking.

Him.

It's all about him.

Endlessly his.

Forever.

Chapter 15

Ayden

The next couple of weeks fly by rather fast. Life begins to return to normal as no more incidents happen with the strange man who broke into the house. The police are still looking for him, but the more days that go by, the less likely it seems that they'll find him.

I hardly spend any time alone anymore. Someone is always with me, except for the rare occasion when I'm driving somewhere by myself, like to therapy. The Gregorys had an alarm installed in their home, which shows how worried they are, not just about the break-in, but because I've been sleep walking more frequently. I think they worry I'll wander off in the middle of the night.

On a positive note, the band is doing pretty fantastic. After our exceptional performance at the opening, Mr. Scott is allowing us to play every other Friday night and wants us to put together some songs to hopefully record in the future months.

And Ethan hasn't mentioned anything about catching Lyric and I mid kiss. I think he does know about the relationship, though, because every time he sees Lyric and I together, a suspicious look crosses his face.

I have therapy once a week after school, both my regular sessions and my amnesia one. After all the sessions, my mind is as empty as it was to begin with. Dr. Gardingdale thinks it's because my fear is blocking my memories. I agree with him, but until I can figure out a way to eliminate that fear, there's not much I can do.

After school, I make the ten-minute drive to the office. We start out with my normal session. Dr. Gardingdale asks me the same questions about how I've been doing, and I give him the same answers. I try to stay away from the Lyric subject, not ready to discuss her with him. Yet I somehow accidentally imply that I'm seeing someone.

"I didn't know you were dating anyone." Across the desk, Dr. Gardingdale gapes at me, stunned.

I shake my head, ready to deny it, but then hesitate. Maybe it's time to tell someone about Lyric and me, get the secret off my chest. Make it more real. Besides, it's not like the doctor can tell anyone.

"Well... I might be, but I just haven't said anything

about it."

"Why not?" His overly bushy brows furrow as he jots something in the legal pad he uses to take notes.

"I don't know… I guess I'm confused and worried." I fiddle with the leather bands on my wrist. Endlessly yours forever. My heart still races just thinking about that night, my emotions a jumble. That night had meant something. To me. To Lyric. To both of us. I'm really falling for her. But I still feel so guilty, still feel unworthy of her.

"Worried and confused about what?" The doctor interrupts my thoughts.

"About how my parents will react." I realize I referred to Mr. and Mrs. Gregory as my parents.

That's a new one… I don't even know what to make of it. What it means about me. That I'm progressing? I shouldn't be so surprised since I'm progressing with Lyric as well.

I trace the cracks in the wooden armrest of the chair I'm sitting in. "And I'm confused because… I don't know, even though I love Lyric's company, I'm still afraid."

"Of what?"

I narrow my eyes at him. "I think we've talked enough

that you know what I'm afraid of."

He drums his pencil on his desk. "I know we've talked about a lot of fears, so I'm not positive which one you're referring to right now."

Even though I know he's trying to heal me, I hate when he makes me say things I don't want to say aloud.

"My fear that I've been sexually abused at some point in my life… At some point when I was in that house. And I'm afraid that I'll never fully be able to get over it—that I'll never be the person Lyric deserves." My fingers curl around the armrests. "I don't know why you make me say it when you already know what I'm going to say."

He scribbles in the notepad the sets the pen down. "Because I believe it's important for you to verbalize them instead of keeping things locked in like you've done in the past."

I roll my tongue in my mouth, aggravated at myself for being so messed up. "So you think it's been a good thing for me to go to this amnesia therapy? I mean, it's gotten me to speak about stuff aloud, even though it hasn't really done anything to strike up the right memories."

"You seem really agitated today."

"I'm agitated every day that I have to come to these

amnesia sessions."

He loosens his tie that has smiley faces on it, conveying happiness that never happens while I'm in these four walls. Our sessions have been about splitting me open and bleeding me dry. Coming here is emotionally exhausting, but as long as Lila and Ethan want me to continue seeing the doctor, I will. They gave me a roof over my head. Got dragged into a police investigation. Got dragged into a mess with a group of people who worship evil.

"You shouldn't push yourself too hard." He gathers a large blue mug from his desk and takes sip of coffee. "If it's becoming too much for you to handle then it's too much for you to handle."

"The police aren't really giving me a choice." I anxiously jiggle my leg up and down. "Well, they are, but if I don't do it, I'm pretty much refusing to help track down my brother's killers… and the people who tried to ruin my life. They've been really pushy, too, calling Lila all the time and asking for reports."

"I'll suggest he not call so much the next time I speak to Detective Rannali. He needs to understand that these things can't be rushed and that it takes time." His phone vibrates on the desk, and he silences it without checking the screen. "How are things going with the Gregorys? You haven't really said much about them lately."

"They're going good. I feel bad that they have to go through all this stuff, but they seem okay with it for some reason." It feels late, well past the normal hour I usually spend here. Out the window, twilight has risen and kissed the sky with silver stars. Usually our session ends before the sun fully sets. "Did we run late today? Shouldn't we be starting the amnesia therapy already?"

"Yes, but Lila just requested that I spend an extra hour with you today before we delve into that." His phone hums again. This time he picks it up and presses a few buttons. "She felt that with everything going on, you might need some extra time to discuss how you're feeling."

"How I'm feeling about what?" Removing my keys out of my pocket, I trace the jagged edge of across the palm of my hand, trying to channel my restless energy stemming from knowing that shortly we'll be trying to crack open my head.

He sets down the phone and overlaps his hands on his desk. "The fear that your capturers might still be out there."

"That's not a new revelation. I've always known they

were out there."

"I know, but in a way, the loss of your brother has brought the memory of that back into your life. And the incident with the break-in—it has to be hard to deal with."

"The police don't know for sure if our kidnappers were the ones who killed my brother or broke into my house." A lump swells in my throat at the mention of my brother's death.

"I also heard you played your first concert." He avoids my statement. "That had to be stressful."

"Not really. Playing relaxes me more than anything. Lyric was pretty nervous, though."

"Lyric, the girl you're dating?" he asks, even though he knows her. Not only because I talk about her sometimes, but because she had a session with him after William assaulted her.

I nod. "That would be the Lyric I'm talking about."

He opens a file and glances at a paper inside. "Does she know what's going on with you at all?"

I nod again. Lyric knows more than most people. Maybe even more than my therapist.

"Do you talk to her about your past a lot?" he asks,

shutting the folder.

"Sometimes."

"About what exactly?"

"Everything I can."

He meticulously examines my expression over, hunting for cracks in my façade. Like always, I grow uneasy. What does he see? A broken shell of a guy that may never be fixed?

My phone abruptly vibrates from inside my pants pocket, giving me an excuse to look away from his scrutinizing gaze.

Lila: Hey, when is your therapy going to be done? I want to know when I should start dinner.

Me: We should be starting the amnesia therapy soon. It usually only takes about fifteen minutes.

Lila: K. See u soon. And drive careful, sweetie.

"We should wrap this up." I stand up and stretch my arms above my head, ready to get the next part over. "It's getting late and Lila needs me home anyway."

"Alright, lie down on the sofa then." He motions at the leather couch nestled in the corner of the room near his filing cabinet and the window.

The ceiling has an unpainted spot where the plaster

shows through. I don't know why, but whenever I lie down, I always find myself picturing it caving in and the sheet-rock raining down on me.

The doctor turns on some mellow music, a symphony of violins. Then he turns on the camera, sits down in a chair in front of me, and clicks on a timer.

"Close your eyes, Ayden," he begins with a droning tone. "You're in a safe place, where no one can hurt you. Now, let your mind relax."

Like always, I fleetingly feel like I'm falling.

Down.

Down.

Down.

Then I crash into a wall.

You can't think about it.

You aren't allowed.

There was a reason for your amnesia.

You think we'd let you off that easy.

You think we'd really let you go.

Don't think too much.

Or you're going to lose control.

We're going to come after you.

Dark eyes... thin bodies.... yellow teeth... blue and red lights flash as sirens get closer to the home. Someone is banging on the door, shouting, "Open up!"

My sister lifts her head and there's life in her eyes for the first time. My brother is curled up in the corner, though, thin, frail, so close to death.

Our capturers flee, but not without an impending warning.

"No one escapes," a woman whispers as she stabs her fingernails into my hands. "We'll come back for you." Her face... blurred... but the pain... is excruciating.

My eyelids spring open to the patch on the ceiling. The room is quiet, but my heart thunders like a storm inside my chest.

Dr. Gardingdale waits patiently at my side with pen and paper in his hand and hope in his eyes that I'll tell him I remembered the identities of the people.

"I saw a few images, but everyone's faces are blurred over, and honestly, none of what I'm seeing makes sense," I tell him as I sit up and plant my feet on the floor. As usual, the room twirls around me in hazy colors and shapes. "They threatened us, though, when we left the house. Said they'd come back for us." Invisible fingers wrap around my neck and my oxygen supply dwindles. "You should proba-bly tell the police that. Or I will."

He nods his head at the camera. "They'll see this when I give them the video tomorrow."

I massage my aching chest. "Did I say anything aloud to you by chance?"

He sighs heavily. "Unfortunately no, which I find strange, especially considering you've been sleep walking and talking so much at home. It's like your mind opens up after the sessions."

"Is that common?"

"It's hard to say." He removes his glasses and cleans them off with the bottom of his shirt. "This therapy—hypnotherapy as a lot call it—isn't something performed that frequently. And your case is extremely complex." He slides his glasses back on. "But, Ayden, if this doesn't start working... I... there might be some other treatments you might consider trying... they're a bit more experimental and have risks, though."

My brows furrow. "What kinds of experimental treat-ments?"

He pushes his feet against the floor, wheeling his chair

back toward a printer. Then he collects a thin stack of papers and hands them to me.

"Shock treatment." Words jump out at me from the pages. Ice cold water. Injections. Electricity.

"They're risky procedures," he explains, looking as though he doesn't really want to be discussing this with me. "I honestly don't believe it's a great idea, but I want to give you the choice. I think that's important. Just like I know it's important to you to find out who killed your brother." When I don't respond, he sighs. "You can throw them away if you want to. I just want you to be informed. Since you're still a minor, though, I can't do anything without your parents' consent, so you'll have to talk to your parents."

"I'll be eighteen in a couple of weeks," I tell him, even though I want to throw the papers away.

Some of the treatments are appalling. But as I think of my brother lying dead in his own blood outside that home that stripped us bare, I fold the papers up and stand up to leave.

"I better go. It's getting late."

"Ayden," he calls out. I pause, twisting around. "Remember, if you ever need to talk, I'm here. Even when it's not a session, you can always call me."

I bob my head up and down then exit the office, pretending his words don't affect me as much as they do. But the fact that I have people in my life who care about me still gets to me and makes me feel warm and cold inside. Warm, because it's amazing to have people in your life rooting for you. And cold, because it's terrifying having people in your life, putting themselves in harm's way to help you.

My thoughts drift to my brother who probably had no one in his life. Who died all by himself.

"Why were you there?" I whisper to myself as I enter the crisp night. The moon is crescent in the dusky sky and a haze conceals most of the stars. "Was it because they had you against your will?"

A depressing thought occurs to me. I might never get the answers to those questions. I might never know what happened to my brother.

But I can still find out about my sister. If I can find her.

On my way to the car, I check my email on my phone, hoping there's a message from Rebel Tonic. Almost three weeks later and still no word from him, I've pretty much lost hope that he'll ever get back to me. More than likely he played me, and like a sucker, I fell for it.

No new messages so I stuff the phone away and speed up across the vacant parking lot. The sole lamppost that usually lights up the area has burnt out so I can scarcely make out the outline of my black BMW. As I find my way through the dark and approach the vehicle, I pat my pocket for my keys but can't find them. Wondering if I left them in the building, I flip around to head back inside. Mid turn I notice something in the trees lining the property. Movement? A figure moving? I can't quite tell.

I dodge to the right and skitter for the door. It has to be a dog or something. No need to get paranoid. With everything that's happened over the last couple of months, my mind's just playing tricks on me.

Then I hear a bloodcurdling scream reverberate from nearby.

Fuck, dogs don't scream.

Freezing, I scan the trees, the closed stores across the street, and the office building, but I can't see anyone or anything around. I jog for the door, my boots thumping against the pavement. As I reach the curb, I hear another scream. This time the noise fractures my heart into a thousand pieces.

This time I recognize the scream.

"Sadie?" I frenziedly whirl around again. Branches snap and leaves rustle. I fumble for my phone as I inch toward the tree line, prepared to dial nine-one-one if needed. "Sadie, are you in there?" I call out as the tips of my boots reach the border of where the parking lot shifts to a shallow forest. I squint through the darkness, but it's pitch black. Too fucking dark.

Darkness settles

a heavy quilt

suffocating.

I can't breathe.

Whisper the words,

They say,

Whisper them and we'll free you.

Whisper.

Whisper.

Whisper

that you worship us.

Belong to us.

That you'll do anything for us.

We're coming back for you.

I swipe my finger to unlock my phone and illuminate the screen. Then I aim the light toward the forest. A screech echoes from amongst the thick leaves then a figure zips from the trees at me. I stumble back, clumsily drop the phone, and darkness smothers me.

Find the fucking phone.

Footsteps rush around in soft pitter-patters.

I collapse to my knees.

Find the fucking phone.

"Ayden, Ayden, Ayden," a low chant echoes around me. "You think we'd let you get away that easy?"

Ayden, Ayden, Ayden,

do you hear us calling your name?

Feel the cuffs around your wrists.

We own you now, Ayden,

there's no getting out, even when you leave these walls.

Ayden, Ayden, Ayden,

Do you see what we can do?

Do you see the blood that stains the ground?

If you leave, we'll come after you.

"Ayden, Ayden, Ayden." Whispers mix with the wind.

"We have her. Your sister. And we're coming for you."

"It's just your imagination." I cover my ears with my hands. "You're just remembering again. Nothing is happening... Nothing... There's nothing out there."

I feel a tug on my hair, strands getting ripped out, then nothing. With a deep breath, I lift open my eyelids. Nothing but darkness and trees and I lower my hands from my ears.

"Ayden." A voice slams up from behind me.

I stagger to my feet and spin around, only to find Dr. Gardingdale standing there with shock frozen on his face. "Where did you..." I reel back around. The area is silent. The trees still. As if nothing happened. "I don't..." My mind races a million miles a minute.

What the hell just happened?

Did I just imagine it?

Or was it real?

They said they're coming back for you, like they did when you were pulled out of that house. Is this it? Are they returning to me? But then, why taunt me instead of taking me? Why scare me, rip out a chunk of my hair, and break into my house to take my knife? Is this part of the ritual? And what is the ritual for?

"What's wrong?" he asks as he surveys the parking lot then the forest. "Did you see something out there?"

I face him and shift my weight so the trees are in my peripheral vision. Then I give the doctor a recap of what I think I just saw, trying to explain to him the best I can.

"It could have been a homeless person or some kids messing around." He scratches his balding head as he stares at the trees and shrubbery. "Both have caused commotions around here before."

"But they said my name." I lower myself onto the curb and drop my head in my hands. "Or at least I think they did… Maybe that was just part of a memory surfacing. Maybe the amnesia therapy was delayed or something." I grip the back of my neck. "I don't know though. I thought they pulled my hair. And it actually hurts right now."

"Pulled your hair?" A pucker forms at his brow. "I think we should at least report the incident to the police, just to be on the cautious side." He sits down on the curb next to me. "I wish you'd have told me how bad the memories were—that you were having a hard time grasping reality while they are happening."

"It's never been that bad before." I raise my head and stare out at the cars on the road ahead of us.

"It might be wise if I prescribe you something," he suggests. "Just until you get a better grappling with remembering."

"I'm not taking drugs," I reply in a clipped tone. But after seeing my mother turn into a monster when she was doped up, I made a vow never to use drugs of any kind.

"It's just a mild sedative that you can take if you have another episode." He pushes to his feet and cautiously moves toward the trees. "You don't have to take it all the time, only when needed." He bends over and scoops something up before returning to me. "Let's go inside so we can report this." He hands me the object he picked up—my phone. "Then we'll call Lila."

I follow him back inside his office, take a seat in the chair, and listen to him recount what happened to the police. Everything that "allegedly" or "possibly" happened. I agree with him to an extent. I'm not positive of what was real after I heard the scream.

The sound could have easily triggered a nerve and sent me to the most vivid places in my mind. Places I never knew existed. But then again, it could be the same person who broke into my house.

One thing I am sure of. I know what I heard. That scream rang familiar to my sister Sadie's. I know her scream well. Heard it day in and day out while we were locked up.

As I wait for Dr. Gardingdale to finish the police call, I check my email again. The screen is cracked from dropping it onto the asphalt, and I have to press each button at least five times just to get into my inbox. I open the app and hold my breath as I scroll through the messages. My heart stops when I reach the fifth line down in my inbox. A message from Rebel Tonic. I open it, praying that he's been able to find her.

Sorry it took me so long to get this to you. For some reason there was no record of a Sadie Stephorson social service's records. I did manage to track an address through her school records, but it took a long time since there are so many districts. The last place she was listed living at was 40499 Faring Lake Ave. Street in San Diego. Hope that helps and good luck.

P.S. Remember to delete this message from your email when you're finished.

I do a map search on the Internet for the address. It's fairly close to where I am now, on the route home if I take the long way.

I do exactly as he instructed. After I type the address in the note section of the phone, I delete the email. Then I wait very impatiently for the doctor to finish up his call.

After he chats with the police, he calls my parents to update them on what happened. When he hangs up, I receive a text message.

Lila: Ayden, Dr. Gardingdale is going to walk you to your car. Lock the doors and drive straight home. And if you see anything that's suspicious, call me.

I'm getting ready to put the phone away when another text comes through.

Lila: Better yet, just stay there. I'll have Ethan come get u.

Me: I'll be fine. It's a ten minute drive.

Lila: Just check the backseat, okay? Sometimes people can hide back there.

Me: You've been watching too many horror movies.

Lila: Maybe so, but u still need to.

Me: Okay.

I close up my phone then the doctor walks me to my

car, telling me that the police will probably be in touch with me sometime tomorrow after they've done some investigating around the area. He waits near the curb as I check the backseat, climb in, and turn on the engine. Then he starts for the door as I drive out of the parking lot and onto the nearly vacant street.

My fingers thrum restlessly as I steer past stores, houses, and gas stations. The closer I get to the address the more jittery I become.

Ten minutes later, I near the location of the address. I'm not positive what I'm even going to do when I arrive. Knock on the door? I wasn't even supposed to take the detour let alone leave the vehicle. And it feels wrong to put myself into danger by getting out of the car at night in some strange area. I should just drive by then maybe return during daylight. Perhaps bring Lyric with me.

Just a quick peek then it's home for me.

Faring Lake Ave. Street is in a subdivision near a shopping mart and a park. When I turn down the road, the first thing I notice is that a lot of the single story homes are abandoned. A lot of the structures appear old and outdated, paint peeling off the siding, mailboxes knocked down. I don't think too much of it until I pull up to the house with the numbers 40499 next to the door. Like the other homes, this one appears vacant. Shingles are missing from the roof, the porch is collapsing, and the windows are all covered with plywood.

I start to choke up, the wind getting knocked out of me as I turn around and the headlights beam across the home. Painted across the wood, in various colors are circular marks.

Marks that resemble my tattoo.

Chapter 16

Lyric

"You seem really happy," my dad remarks as he stuffs half a roll into his mouth. "Like extra happy."

"You really do," my mother agrees as she adds a glob of butter to her potatoes. "I wonder why." Her tone insinuates something. What, I'm not sure.

Either she's speculating that I might be bipolar, or she's trying to get me to fess up as to why I've been almost stupidly happy over the last couple of weeks.

I shovel a spoonful of corn into my mouth. "I'm a normal happy, you guys, so don't start."

"We weren't starting." My mother works with a knife to slice her steak. "And I'm sorry for ever bringing that up. I'm really sorry about that, Lyric. I should have never said anything."

"Okay, good." I smile at her, and she returns it.

At the moment, all feels right in the world.

Despite all the drama, life has been good, something I ponder as I eat my mashed potatoes.

Things really have been great.

And calm.

As if the world is attempting to prove my thoughts wrong, all hell suddenly breaks loose as the back door flies open and bashes against the doorstopper.

Aunt Lila comes barreling into the kitchen, her eyes massive and jam-packed with terror. "I need you to watch the kids," she sputters to my mother as she winds a scarf around her neck. "Something happened with Ayden at therapy, and he was supposed to come straight home, but it's been over an hour since he left. Ethan's already out looking for him, but I'm going to go check a few places, too."

Fear pulsates through my body. I quickly check my phone to see if there are any messages from Ayden, but I have no new texts.

My mother shoves back from the table, the chair legs making a godawful scratching noise against the hardwood floor. "Let me just grab my coat and I'll be over."

I stand up so abruptly I damn near tip the chair over. "I'm going with you," I say to Lila.

"Okay, that's fine." Aunt Lila is distracted as she glides her finger across the screen of her phone, checking for messages. "I don't know why he's not answering my calls or texts… he never does stuff like this."

"I'll drive around with Lyric, and we can check some places, too," my dad adds as he hurries for the stairs. "Just let me grab my phone and wallet."

I send Ayden a text.

Me: Where the hell r u? Everyone's freaking out.

Then I head to grab my jacket from the coat rack when the back door opens up behind me.

"I found her house," Ayden says to me as he enters the foyer and closes the door.

"You're okay!" I throw my arms around him, unaware until now how worried I was. "Everyone's freaking out." I pull back. "Wait, found who?"

"The last address my sister lived at." His hair is disheveled, there are dark circles are under his eyes, and his shoulders are hunched, as if the weight of the world is crushing him.

"Rebel Tonic got back to you?"

He nods. "With an address."

"And?"

His throat muscles work as he swallows hard and fights back tears. "It was a vacant house with this," he lifts up the bottom of his shirt and taps his finger on the rough tattoo on his side, "painted all over the boarded up windows."

I gulp. "Why… I don't understand."

"Neither do I." He grips ahold of my hand. "But we're going to go find out." He marches across the room toward the kitchen.

"Where are we going?" I ask as I shuffle to keep up with him.

"To my house. I need to talk to Lila to find out what that letter was about."

"Lila's here, in the kitchen. She was about to go look for you," I tell him, which only makes him quicken his pace.

When we enter the kitchen and Aunt Lila sees Ayden, a choking sob wrenches from her throat.

"Oh, my God, we were so worried about you." She crosses the kitchen and wraps her arms around Ayden.

He stands with his listless arms to his sides, still holding my hand. "I need you to tell me what that letter was about." He doesn't have to explain what letter he's speaking of. The reluctant expression on Aunt Lila's face reveals she already knows.

"Ayden, Ethan and I already explained that there's some things you aren't ready for yet," she reminds him sympathetically.

"I tracked her last address down," he states bluntly, firmly holding her gaze. "It was about ten miles away from here. The house is boarded up and has these marks spray painted on it, ones that match my tattoo."

"Ayden..." Her face contorts with emotional agony.

He tugs me closer to his side. "Just tell me."

Aunt Lila seals her quivering lips together as tears fill the corners of her eyes. Ayden's fingers clench around my hand as he watches her unravel in front of us.

"Your sister was kidnapped again not too long after you guys were ... found in that house." She lowers herself into a chair. "She's been with those people for the last two and a half years. The police honestly thought she was dead until they received a note from her over a year ago on the day we brought you home."

"What did the letter say?" he chokes out hoarsely, and I feel him sway, as if his legs are about to buckle.

"I don't know," she replies as tears stream down her cheeks. "The police won't release that information."

"Is that what happened to my brother, too?" he whispers in horror. "Was he kidnapped? Did they kill him?"

"All I know about your brother is what you do. He vanished out of the system a couple of years ago. Social services assumed he'd ran away. The next time he was found..." She reaches out to touch his shoulder, but he moves away. More tears bubble in her eyes. "I'm so sorry."

"Why didn't anyone tell me this?" Ayden starts to sit down even though there's no chair around. I quickly usher him to a nearby barstool before he ends up falling on the floor.

"Because we wanted you to have a normal life." She fights back a sob, her chest heaving as she verges toward hysteria. "Oh, sweetie, I'm so sorry you have to go through this."

She runs over, wraps her arms around him, and squeezes him tightly. Ayden stares like he sees a ghost in the space in front of him, those dark eyes of his completely haunted with his past.

"You're going to be okay," she promises him, smoothing her hand over his head. "We'll get through this. The police are looking for her."

Still clutching onto my hand, my arm ends up getting crushed between their bodies. I wiggle it, but Ayden refuses to let go. Finally, I relax and let him hold on.

"I want to try to remember," he croaks. "Do whatever it takes to find those people... Doctor Gardingdale... he said there were other methods..."

"Yeah, the detective mentioned those to me, too," Lila's tone is uneven, "and they're too risky."

"Leaving my sister with those people, hoping she'll make it out alive is too risky..." His fingers enfold around the back of his neck and grip tight. "I swear I heard her scream in the parking lot tonight... She was there..."

"Oh, honey." She pulls him nearer, like she has no clue what else to do but hang onto him.

I want to stop the pain in his life and make him feel safe, but I don't have that power.

Right now, everything relies on what the people after Ayden want. Until we find out exactly what that is, no one's going to feel safe again.

About the Author

Jessica Sorensen is a *New York Times* and *USA Today* bestselling author that lives in the snowy mountains of Wyoming. When she's not writing, she spends her time reading and hanging out with her family.

Other books by Jessica Sorensen:

The Coincidence Series:

The Coincidence of Callie and Kayden

The Redemption of Callie and Kayden

The Destiny of Violet and Luke

The Probability of Violet and Luke

The Certainty of Violet and Luke

The Resolution of Callie and Kayden

Seth & Grayson (Coming Soon)

The Secret Series:

The Prelude of Ella and Micha

The Secret of Ella and Micha

The Forever of Ella and Micha

The Temptation of Lila and Ethan

The Ever After of Ella and Micha

Lila and Ethan: Forever and Always

Ella and Micha: Infinitely and Always

The Shattered Promises Series:

Shattered Promises

Fractured Souls

Unbroken

Broken Visions

Scattered Ashes

Breaking Nova Series:

Breaking Nova

Saving Quinton

Delilah: The Making of Red

Nova and Quinton: No Regrets

Tristan: Finding Hope

Wreck Me

Ruin Me

The Fallen Star Series (YA):

The Fallen Star

The Underworld

The Vision

The Promise

The Fallen Souls Series (spin off from The Fallen Star):

The Lost Soul

The Evanescence

The Darkness Falls Series:

Darkness Falls

Darkness Breaks

Darkness Fades

The Death Collectors Series (NA and YA):

Ember X and Ember

Cinder X and Cinder

Spark X and Cinder (Coming Soon)

The Sins Series:

Seduction & Temptation

Sins & Secrets

Unbeautiful Series:

Unbeautiful

Unraveling Series:

Unraveling You

Raveling You

Awakening You

Inspiring You (coming soon)

Standalones

The Forgotten Girl

Coming Soon:

Entranced

Steel & Bones

21063534R00149

Printed in Great Britain
by Amazon